John B Carey

The Oddities of Short-Hand

The Coroner and his Friends

John B Carey

The Oddities of Short-Hand
The Coroner and his Friends

ISBN/EAN: 9783337395612

Printed in Europe, USA, Canada, Australia, Japan

Cover: Foto ©Andreas Hilbeck / pixelio.de

More available books at **www.hansebooks.com**

OF

SHORT-HAND;

OR THE

CORONER AND HIS FRIENDS.

BY

JOHN B. CAREY,

With a Preface by TIMOTHY BIGELOW, Esq.

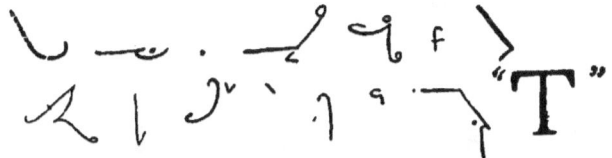

BEING QUAINT AND CURIOUS NARRATIVES TOLD BY
THE WORSHIPPERS AT THE SHRINE OF TRUTH
WITH A CAPITAL "T."

———

In shorthand skilled, where little marks comprise
Whole words, a sentence in a letter lies.
                                    CRABBE.

———

EXCELSIOR PUBLISHING HOUSE.
New York.
AMERICAN NEWS COMPANY. Agents.

DEDICATION.

TO her who bade me look up when I was cast down ; who clothed and fed me when I was naked and hungry ; who aided and soothed me when I was helpless and sorrowful ; who stood by me steadily and loved me always—to my dead but unforgotten Mother, this humble book is affectionately dedicated by the author.

June, 1891.

CONTENTS.

PREFACE.

TO my admiration of the contents of this volume, expressed when I had the pleasure of looking over the typoscript, the reader is perhaps indebted for the poor privilege of reading this introduction. The many favorable opinions expressed as to the merits of this work have doubtless encouraged the author to the point of publication, and have certainly encouraged me to write the preface.

Although the author could say what should be said much better than I, yet I cheerfully comply with his request so as to spare his modesty the bestowal of such praise as the work deserves.

One of the reasons for the assertion that he who is his own lawyer has a fool for a client, is that an advocate can, without censure, make claims for a client which it would be inappropriate, if not immodest, for the client to make for himself, no matter how well founded. It may be that some such logic as this actuated the writer of this volume in his desire to have a preface written by a friendly hand.

The only hesitation I feel in undertaking this task arises from a doubt of my ability to set forth truly the literary merits of the work. I trust, however, that the reader will not stop with this introduction, disappointing as it may be, but persevere to the end, so that he may reap the harvest of profit and pleasure which its pages offer.

A few words as to the scope and objects of the book.

Whether so intended or not, it will serve to extinguish the slander that "the stenographer, from constantly writing the thoughts of others, becomes in time a mere mechanical instrument, incapable of thinking for himself, requiring the spoken thoughts of thinking men to put him in motion, and that therefore, the more he knows of stenography, the less he knows of anything else."

It is not a book on stenography by an advocate of any particular system of swift writing, but one which the adept in the art, the amateur, and the non-phonographic reader can peruse, enjoy, and one in which they mayhap find touches here and there that remind them of Poe, or Twain, or Dickens.

One of the objects of the work is to illustrate the liability to error. The rapid spread of geometrical sound-writing, otherwise, and not so well called, phonography, in the domain of business life within the past decade, has been attended with many incidents grotesque, painful, and perhaps surprising. This might have been anticipated, because employers, as well as employees had to learn how to use a new thing, and the former had, in many cases to accept inexperienced help freshly "turned out" of the schools.

Odd errors of transcription have from time to time furnished occasion for mirth or for anger. Long before the day of phonography the proverb "It is human to err" had met with acceptance. It is therefore obvious that inaccuracies

are not peculiar to short-hand.   Telegraphy
we know has had its share, and ordinary longhand script has at times provoked profanity or
led to disaster.   Of a truth, though, phonography is the more dangerous, because the omissions
necessary to brevity reduce words to the merest
skeletons or outlines, as they are called, and
hence lessen distinctions.   We all know that
the bony structures of our bodies called skeletons are more like to each other than we are
to ourselves in life when the osseous fragments
are clothed in the flesh.   The same bony frame-
work indeed, might serve for the foundation or
scaffolding of entirely different kinds of men,
for a Talmage, an Ingersoll, a Gladstone or a
Claude Duval.

So it is with shorthand.   When we find that
the skeletons of *minister* and of *monster*, of *philosopher* and *falsifier*, of *lawyer* and of *liar* are
alike, we begin to feel that we require means of
distinction and they are accordingly provided,
but alas ! not always observed.

In devising a system of abbreviated writing,
the starting point is the point of the pen or instrument to be employed.   As a line is generated
by the movement of a point, so all shorthand is
generated by the gyrations of the instrument
and consist of the lines traced by it.   Obviously,
if every difference between forms so traceable is
made significant, the resulting signs will possess
their highest representing power ; *ergo*, fewer of
them will do a given work; less time will be required to make them, and hence speed will be
increased.

This principle has been carried to an extreme

in some of the systems of phonography. Thus the size of the character which in ordinary script is immaterial, is made much of in shorthand. In longhand the form is all significant although form too is quite essential in phonography. The aim has been for the sake of speed to have forms as simple as possible, accordingly each letter consists of a single dot or stroke. Dots are made significant by position, and are assigned to vowel representation.

The consonants with which the art mainly deals are represented by strokes, straight or curved, and differentiated by direction. Each of the three sizes and several forms made in various directions, perpendicular, sloping to the left, the right, and horizontal, give only twelve characters; yet, by making a distinction of thickness, their availability is increased, and there are just about enough of them to represent the consonants. Not alone are size, form, direction, and thickness made significant, but also the position of the characters with reference to each other and the line of writing. All these matters require consideration by the writer, and a failure in any of them may lead to doubt. The doubt may be resolved by the context, by the knowledge of the writer as to his own peculiarities and inaccuracies when writing rapidly, or by a concentrated study of the doubtful character. As flourishes are not permissible, each sign means something; there is some word in the language which, being suggested, may be seen at once to be that for which the character was intended, and often beyond the possibility of error. But until the illuminating suggestion comes well may he exclaim :

"But that large grief which these enfold
Is given in outline, and no more."

Even with the aid of the context, knowledge
of the subject and his own peculiarities, the
writer of notes is often puzzled by a symbol
which another may decipher at sight.   The one
has the key to the lock in his mental grasp, the
other has not.

Having indicated the possibilities of error in
phonography, it may be imagined that there
lurks in it a vast potency for mischief.   Written
with a pencil these possibilities are increased,
and are still more augmented by haste and carelessness.

Now whatever *may* happen is to be taken into
account, as well as what *has* happened. That the
author had such a thought in mind in the writing of some of these sketches I have reason to
believe; nor am I loath to say that he has worked
out the idea, and presented the possible in a
peculiarly quaint and interesting way, wherein
humor and pathos are fairly blended.

The story which appeared some years ago in
a newspaper about the escape of the savage animals at Central Park and their dreadful destruction of human life ; the account of the dashing
of a ferry-boat into the slip at full speed, and
its consequent destruction and the maiming of
many persons, because of the sudden illness of
the pilot, were better than true, for they led to
such precautions as may prevent their ever happening.

Indeed, there is a kind of truth which is in no
case a statement of fact ; and, it may be doubted
whether there ever was a statement which em-

bodied the whole truth and nothing but the truth.

When Hamlet says " As easy as lying," it might seem to mean that it is difficult to tell the truth ; and so it is, if it means a statement in exact conformity to facts. If it means to relate our impressions from observation it is not difficult.

But as there are sounds which we cannot hear, and rays of light not perceptible to our eyes, so there is a truth not of seeing or hearing, but of experience, organization and reflection—a truth which depends upon the mental as well as the physical conditions of perception. The metaphorical rose-colored spectacles may not be placed before the physical eye, but serve as a screen behind " the windows of the soul," incorporated into the substance of the sentient nerve itself, or made part of its mode of action ; so that even the truth of simple vision is not demonstrably the same to any two of us. " There is, moreover, a truth of fiction more veracious than the truth of fact, as that of the poet which represents to us things and events rather than servilely copies them as they are imperfectly imaged in the crooked and smoky glass of our mundane affairs."

These considerations may serve to give an idea of the kind of truth the votaries spoken of in this volume worshiped—the imaging of that which might have happened with " Short hand as she is wrote," not classically or with the absolute correctness always-desirable and seldom attained, but with the dash and hurry required by the exigencies of business ; and the reader is

cordially recommended to close his hypercriti-
cal eyes and open his mental capacities to the
full and unquestioning acceptance thereof.

TIMOTHY BIGELOW,

City Court of Brooklyn.

June, 1891

CHAPTER I.

THE WORSHIPERS AND THE SHRINE.

MR. NORTHCOATE was slowly making his way to the flat, that is, the apartment house, on the fourth floor of which he resided. The other tenants of the building, the Coroner, Engineer Whitcomb, Mr. Grace, a Real Estate Dealer, and a Lawyer in the adjoining flat, were accustomed to meet Mr. Northcoate in one of the suite of rooms occupied by the owner of the premises.

To this trysting place Mr. Northcoate was going. One evening each week was devoted by the gentlemen mentioned to reminiscences, smoking tobacco and swapping exaggerations in the host's cozy lounging room. These six gentlemen were simply members of an unorganized social club, a club without dues, constitution, by-laws, officers, or name, the members of which were known to each other as worshipers at the shrine of truth, with a very large T.

Northcoate was a court reporter, and, like all of his class, a gentleman of extreme leisure; his whole effort in life had been to kill time. Hurry was a thing he was quite incapable of. His walk was the slow, stately, dignified tread peculiar to sick turtles and fat policemen. Haste was a thing utterly unknown to him. His daily business, if he did anything, was simply to go into court, sometimes even in the morning, sit quietly at a desk and make little marks. The lawyers, judges and witnesses did all the hard work of talking, and it did not require a very strong man to perform Northcoate's labor—perhaps we should say recreation.

He sauntered slowly up the steps of the house, rang the bell, and, when the door was opened, entered what the Real Estate Man called the "Snuggery."

He found there the other gentlemen chatting, as they sat in various attitudes and altitudes.

The Engineer had his slippered feet upon the marble mantelpiece over the grate fire. The Coroner was lolling back in a rocking chair, watching the blue smoke as it curled up from a rather aged looking brierwood ; the Host and the Real Estate Dealer sat in armchairs, each with a leg thrown over the arm. The Lawyer straddled another chair, with the back of it in front of him, on which he rested his folded arms.

The Engineer was a typical Yankee, with the chinwhisker, toothpick and drawl. He could expectorate with marvelous accuracy. He was "off" service in the Selineville & Mudchunk R. R. Co. on account of sickness, and having been "subbed" for a few days, was resting himself in his favorite position in his friend's apartment.

Occupying the second flat the engineer was at home wherever he went, and he was now quietly waiting for the seance or flow of soul that had been provided for this evening.

The Coroner, short, round, with considerable aplomb, and grey eyes that sparkled behind his gold rimmed glasses, was quite the reverse of the railroad man. An indifferent listener, he was the conscious possessor of a mine of narra-

tives from his own personal experience that was
seemingly inexhaustible. He always began "I
remember once," and then you were in for it.
The Coroner was an Irishman, educated, witty,
polished and inclined to be cynical. His horror
of what he called "rum" and the rum traffic
was only equalled by his intense affection for
the weed. He had been thrice elected coroner,
and his professional duties brought him in
close proximity to the lower strata of society,
"in the slums and alleys of a great sinful city."

The pictures he drew of gaunt poverty, willful
murder, unexplained suicide, the ghastly morgue,
the police court and the hospital, were startling,
vivid and gruesome.

A word as to the others. The Host was a
gentleman of leisure who having accumulated a
fair share of this world's goods was content to
stop at the age of two score and ten and take
life easy. Hard-headed and matter of fact ;
with him seeing was believing often, though not
always. It was occasionally necessary in order
to convince him to put the proposition under
discussion in such shape as to appeal to all his
senses. He was ironical, sarcastic to the highest degree, and withal thoroughly enjoyed these
gatherings of his friends on Friday evenings.

In marked contrast was the Real Estate Man,
Somewhat taciturn, this gentleman's forte was
listening. He claimed to be of mediocre mental ability and limited education, and accepted.
or pretended to believe everything he heard,
though he had been known to say in a moment
of great confidence that his motive for acquiescence was that agreement was easier than argu-

ment. "No man," he said, "is ever convinced in a dispute, his friendship is often lost thereby. Concurrence is cheaper than Controversy, and if I don't agree, I pretend to."

He had, moreover, a very pleasant way of listening with great interest to learned discussions on sublimated subjects which he did not understand, and the happy faculty of throwing in a suitable monosyllable such as "Indeed," "Certainly," "Oh, yes," "Surely," that pleased the talkers who always gave him credit for the possession of considerable knowledge concerning things of which, he admitted, he had a vast fund of ignorance.

While not of the boastfully disparaging kind, this gentleman's self-admitted dullness was in reality a mere cloak under which was hidden a deal of what is called "horse sense," and more than an ordinary share of book knowledge.

The Stenographer was a man of but superficial knowledge for one of his calling. Men of his profession, he asserted, never knew enough, for when a Stenographer has thoroughly mastered surgery so as to be prepared for a malpractice case, it is his fate perhaps to be called, professionally, into a patent suit involving mechanical niceties in the construction of a steam engine ; or, having read up on mechanical contrivances from the Barker Mill to automatic switches, he is employed mostly in cases involving profound questions of ecclesiastical jurisprudence or canon law. Coming into contact with so many subjects of which he has little or no knowledge, he rarely profits by the Emersonian advice to not allow things you do not know to hamper your knowledge of the things you do know.

No man in the profession ever knows enough (except of course the amateur), and there was never but one who was thoroughly up in every science and every art.   He mastered it all from the study of theology, astronomy and the occult sciences downwards, and was fully and perfectly equipped to grapple with anything that came to him professionally.

"And did—" replied the deeply interested Host, to whom the other made these remarks.   "No," said the Stenographer softly, "he died."

"Of super-braincranium," suggested the coroner with a twinkle in his little grey eyes.

"I believe so," answered the other; "it was a most deplorable case.   The person I refer to had climbed the dizziest heights of Parnassus, traversed every foot of the field of knowledge, fitted himself by long years of constant and profound study to comprehend thoroughly everything that might come in his way; thus steeped in erudition and crammed with knowledge, he was called upon to report a case of assault and battery, and singularly enough found that he had forgotten how to write shorthand!   The mortification of this discovery killed him."

While the sensation which this awful recital evoked is subsiding, let us glance at the latest but by no means the least important member of the company.

Differing from the others, the Lawyer was an all-around literary athlete, thoroughly up in many things, and while a ripe scholar he was still an industrious student.   After many years spent in gathering information he had reached what is called by some the pinnacle of knowledge—an appreciation of one's ignorance. He required but collision with the intellect of others to bring out his latent powers, and then you had him at his best.

The Counsellor had two points of weakness—or of strength—as you may view it. One was an intense passion for old and much worn books, a passion which despite his constant and persistant assiduity to gratify, was never sated. Another of the learned gentleman's peculiarities was an inordinate liking for that humble offspring of the Southern negro's necessities which has been duly adopted and endorsed by a great President of the United States of America—the corncob pipe.

After the entrance of Mr. Northcoate the meeting opened. The conversation of those in the room shifted but never lagged. At an easy bound it went from China to Electricity and then to Pallindromes.

"Taylor's" the Host was remarking, "I believe has never been equalled, 'Evil did I dwell'; reversed it reads, 'Lewd did I live.' Of course that's fair, but what Adam said to Eve has the brevity of wit, and is exactly the same both ways, 'Madam, I'm Adam.'"

The Lawyer ventured, "Well, I always thought the one ascribed to Napoleon was the best of all. It is related that toward the end of his life he was asked if at any time he could have invaded England, to which he replied: 'Able was I ere I saw Elba.' How's that?"

"Pshaw," said the Coroner, contemptuously,

"that's too venerable," at which the Real Estate Man ejaculated, "Of course."

Then Northcoate spoke of a professional associate, who being ill, was visited by a learned physician. After the usual preliminaries made and provided, that is, feeling the patient's pulse, taking the temperature, noting in his diary a \$3 charge for the visit, etc., the doctor said "Are you sick?" The poor reporter stretched out his hand, he was suffering from incipient tetanus (commonly called lock-jaw) and seizing his pencil from the table wrote:

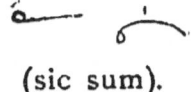

(sic sum).

"Well," snapped the little Coroner, " what of that ?"

"The point of it is," said the other quietly, "did the sick man mean it to be in Latin or in English ?"

"Gracious" interposed the Coroner, "how dreadfully silly ; but, talking about notes, I re member once——"

The others sat back in listening attitudes.

CHAPTER II.

THE CORONER'S NOTES.

" I REMEMBER once," the Coroner went on, " a most singular thing of which that reminds me, concerning notes taken by a young man who acted as my clerk some thirteen years ago. As I said, he was young. Very. It was during my first term of office at one of the first criminal cases I had to do with officially, and at the time, I am free to confess, I was rather young myself.

Word came from Police headquarters that a farm hand on Benton's homestead had been discovered mortally wounded in a small piece of woods not far from the farm.

It was necessary that I should proceed at once to the scene and take the ante-mortem statement of the dying man. That was my official duty, and my clerk and myself started at once for the scene of the assault. Arriving there, we found the injured party, one John Simonetti, an Italian farm laborer, dreadfully wounded about the head and unconscious. He was in a state of coma till shortly after our arrival. While the village physician was laboring to restore him to consciousness, I endeavored, as in duty bound, to get what information I could concerning the occurrence. It was meagre enough. No one had really witnessed it. As usual in such cases, there

was supposed to be a woman in it, a housemaid
on a neighboring farm. A fellow named Peter
Mari, a countryman and cousin of the injured
man, was suspected of having committed the
assault in a fit of jealous rage. He was a tall,
raw-boned, sinister-looking fellow, and I was
against him from the first, and believed him
guilty, although I hadn't a particle of proof.
He claimed to be entirely ignorant of the whole
affair, and was seemingly, at least, solicitous as
to the injured man's condition, attentive about
the bedside, and endeavored to aid the village
doctor as best he could.

All the information I obtained amounted to
nil. It was mostly made up of village gossip
' hearing Mrs. So-and-so say that she heard So-
and-so tell So-and-so that she heard,' etc. ; and
' I think,' and ' says I to myself, says I,' etc.,
etc.

The simple fact was that the man was hurt,
and, as we thought at the time, mortally, and if
he could throw no light on it, no one else could.
Of course, the only proper thing to be done
under the circumstances was to take the ante-
mortem statement ; and when the injured man
exhibited the least sign of intelligence, we proceeded to do this. The task was rendered
difficult because of the poor knowledge the
patient had of the English language, and hence
he could not think of the proper expression to
convey his meaning, and, while seemingly conscious, he was scarcely able to articulate. When
he spoke at all, it was in a mere guttural
whisper. Consequently I directed my clerk to
place his ear close to the patient's lips, in order

to hear even the few tones he could utter. To
do this he had to bend over the bed in an uncomfortable and undignified manner that I
thought quite beneath me.   I had another
reason for this : I had a few questions to which
I wished answers, and I desired, while putting
them, to keep a sharp eye on Mari, in order to
discover, if possible, any indication of guilt on
his strongly marked features.   I thought it well
to write the questions, and taking out my pre-
scription book (an ordinary paper pad about
three inches by four) I wrote the interrogatories
—each on a separate slip or sheet of the pad—
which I stood up and read slowly and distinctly,
to the injured man, all the while watching Mari,
as I told you, in the endeavor to discover the
appearance of the guilt which I firmly believed
existed.   Then I gave the pad to the clerk to
take the answers on, it being more convenient
for him to use in his awkard position, and he
recorded all the answers on the outside, or upper
sheet.   Of course, I should *not* have delegated
the duty of recording the all-important words of
the dying man to my subordinate.   My only
excuse for this is that it was one of my first
cases, my ears were not as good as my clerk's—
certainly not as large—and, as I say, I did not
care to assume the uncomfortable attitude that
he was obliged to take in order to hear the
wounded man's monosyllables.   I watched Mari,
hoping to get evidence sufficient to hold him, as,
having, as I say, taken a dislike to him from the
first, I wished if possible to bring him to justice.
I made the mistake of many young persons who
have to do professionally with criminal cases,

that is to say, I went into it with a prejudice. My great error was in trusting my clerk.

As I told you, I stood up and read each ques- tion, trying to catch the dying man's response. In this I failed, but as my clerk seemed to be writing something on the upper sheet of the pad which I gave him, while he bent over the wounded man, I was satisfied that nothing was lost. I even congratulated myself on his valuable as- sistance ; he was taking notes, as I had instructed him not to lose a syllable uttered by Simonetti. Before the written questions were put, I should have stated that I prefaced them by informing Simonetti that in all probability he would not live ; but it was the lot of all men to die ; he would die to-day, we would die to-morrow, and that it would be well, having made his peace with God, to state what he knew of the occur- rence, fully and frankly. We have a certain form for use on such occasions, which I went through with, and I honestly endeavored to make the approach of death to the dying man as easy as possible. Whether it was that he understood me, or whether it was that his intense suffering made him wish for the end, I will not pretend to say ; but I think he welcomed it, if I could judge by an indescribable lighting up or look of intelligence on his ghastly coun- tenance. During the reading I kept one eye on the man I suspected. I repeat this because I have thought since that I did not give as much attention as I should have given to the most im- portant part of the ante-mortem, to wit : the words of the dying man. The patient was un- able to answer fully, despite repeated efforts made by both my clerk and myself, and we were obliged to be content with the little we obtained. The clerk then handed me the pad, on the upper sheet of which he had taken the answers to the questions in his short hand notes (God bless the mark), and as an ante-mortem statement I endorsed it on either the left or right margin, I don't know which, but I think the right, as follows : 'Ant. M. of Simonetti, t'kn by C., *ex rel.* Mari, Jan. 29, '77,' placed it on top of the slips I had read from, numbered the questions, and putting a light rubber band about the sheets, inclosed them in an envelope with the proper indorsement, and laid it aside to await results.

As I afterwards discovered, I had numbered the slips of the pad containing the questions on one corner before reading, and it may be also that I did an unusual thing for a man who writes an odd screed for the newspapers—it may be, I say, that owing to my nervousness or anxiety, instead of laying the first sheet face down on the table, and the others in the same order on top of it, it is possible that I placed it in the reverse order, face up, and the other above it in the same order, so that when I took them up the numerical order of the interrogatories was reversed, and when I put the sheet containing the clerk's notes on top of mine, I raised one corner, and, not remembering that I had already paged the slips containing my questions, I renumbered them on an opposite corner. This I found out afterwards—the handwriting, of course, was mine, and the paging of each slip was mine.

When we had finished our official business, I bade the dying man cheer up, for although I had but little hope of his recovery, the village physician seemed to think that he had a fighting chance for his life ; and, under the circumstances, we departed without taking any further steps in the matter."

The coroner paused here while he re-lit his pipe.   After a thoughtful whiff or two, he resumed :

" Well, do you know, that man didn't die after all, but he became insane by reason of some obscure injury to the brain, and was placed among the incurables at the Steadville Asylum, where he still remains.   That ended that chapter. Sometime afterwards the Grand Jury of the County, without anything but mere suspicion, but, as I always thought, on generally sound principles, indicted Mari for felonious assault, with intent to kill.   My clerk and myself were subpœnaed to attend the trial at the Court of Sessions, having been served with a subpœna ' Duce Takem,' which means, in plain English, ' bring all the papers relating to the subject under the investigation that you can lay your hands on.'   That, I may say, is a free hand translation.   After we had been subpœnaed, my clerk asked for the proceedings, and I handed him the envelope endorsed, ' Ant. M. Simonetti,' etc.

Shortly afterwards he came to me with a very odd look on his face.   ' Coroner,' he says, ' you numbered these questions in one corner.'   I said, ' of course.   Isn't that proper ?'   ' But,' he went on, ' you also numbered them in the opposite

corner and in the reverse order.' 'Oh, well,' I
said, 'it can't matter much.' 'Do you remember,' he said, 'in which order you read them?' I
looked at them, and I confess I could not
positively tell; you see the double paging on
the opposite corners bothered me some, but I
believe I had read them in the order which I
will show you directly. I said, however, that it
was a matter of very little moment, and that
the answers which he had taken would unerr-
ingly indicate the order of the questions.

The clerk sat down at the desk again, and
after pondering a while he approached me again,
saying, 'Do you remember, sir, on which edge
of the sheet I gave you you indorsed the statement, 'Ant. M. of Simonetti, t'kn by C.,' etc.,
as I handed it to you; whether on the right side
or the left side, that is to say, whether it was
this way?

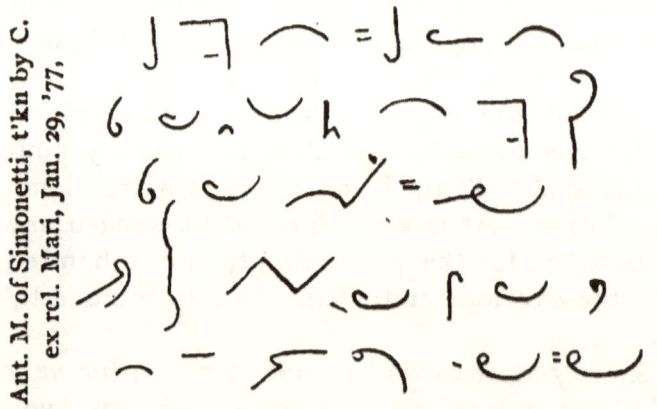

Ant. M. of Simonetti, t'kn by C.
ex rel. Mari, Jan. 29, '77,

or this way?' and he turned the paper upside
down.

Ant. M. Simonetti t'kn by C. ex rel. Mari, Jan. 29, '77.

'Why, of course not,' I said, in surprise. 'You might as well ask me what time I got out of bed any day last month. What difference can it make? It says plainly enough, 'Ante-mortem, Jan. 29th, '77,' and it is my writing; that ought to be conclusive.' He went off with an unsatis-fied look upon his face. In less than a minute he was back again. 'Oh,' he said, 'you didn't place those sheets face down as you read them, did you?' There was something in the man's tone that sounded odd. I began to think he had been drinking, and I looked at him, and looked hard. 'Why,' I said, 'what is the matter with you? Do you suppose I can remember such little things as that? I don't know, and I don't care; you are too anxious about trifles.' 'Oh,' he said, with a short, hard laugh, 'not at all, I only wanted to know, you know.'

I left the office soon afterwards, and although at the time I thought it strange that he should ask me such foolish questions, the whole thing soon passed out of my mind. It all came back to me when I attended court on the following day as a witness.

As I already told you, Mari was placed on trial for assault with intent to kill, and we attended court.

The case of the people was fairly presented. The servant woman testified that she knew the accused, and related little instances tending to show that he was of a jealous, revengeful disposition. The injured man she had not seen for two or three days before the assault, but the accused had visited her that evening, leaving about five o'clock. The fact that Mari was the first to discover the injured man was conclusively shown, Mari himself testifying to it ; and the constable said that the time at which he was notified by Mari was about nine o'clock. The village physician, in describing the condition of the wounds, gave it as his opinion that the injured man had been first struck by a blunt instrument in the back of the head, after which the stabbing or cutting was done. A stableman, a co-employe of the accused, swore that he heard Mari threaten some one, he could not say whom, the night preceding the assault when he was in the stable. My evidence was of little account. I identified the handwriting of the questions ; said I had watched the accused while they were being read, but that I saw no positive indication of guilt in the demeanor of the prisoner at the injured man's bedside. I said, also, that I had not heard any words uttered by the injured man, owing to his weak, almost unconscious state, and referred to the fact that my clerk, in whom I had the utmost confidence, had his ear close to the injured party's lips, and I was confident that what he had put down was what had been said by the injured man, and all of it, but that, so far as I knew, there had been no positive identification of the prisoner. The prisoner's counsel, singularly enough, asked me just the same questions which my clerk had put to me previously, that is, as to which end of the clerk's slips I had made the indorsement on ; whether I had placed my questions face down or face up, and how it occurred that I had paged them double and in reverse order and in opposite corners. On these points, of course, I could throw no light; it having been a matter of indifference to me it had escaped my memory. The fact that the lawyer's questions were substantially the same as the clerk's I supposed was a mere coincidence. The clerk then produced the record, being the interrogatories on the slips that I had read, and the answers I had recorded, and I verily believe this is the order in which I read them. As you observe, the sheets in my handwriting are numbered in the upper right-hand and in the lower left-hand corners."

The Coroner here took from his pocket a large red diary, and taking out several slips of paper, he laid them on the table so that we could read them with the appended answers that had been, as he said, transcribed from his clerk's notes and read on the trial :

1. "Can you give any account of the assault or state what you did or said when you were attacked ?"

A. "Don't cut me. Don't kill me."

2. "Was this man one of your assailants—can you indentify him by his talk ?"

A. "That is one beyond any doubt. Him cut throat."

3. "Are you positive that this was one of them?"

A. "That is one of them—Mari—Cousin."

4. "Was the instrument used, a knife?"

A. "Razor."

5. "Was the motive robbery?"

A. "Think it was robbery."

6. "Was he there alone, or were there more than one?"

A. "One tall. One short."

7. "Could you identify the man, or give the authorities any information as to his character?"

A. "Might get record, sir, of Sing Sing."

"This record, with the other proof adduced, made a strong case against the accused, and the people 'rested.' The prisoner's counsel then opened the case for the accused, and said that he would show conclusively that the injured man had stated positively and unequivocally in his so-called deposition that the prisoner was not guilty. As to the manner in which it would be shown he preferred to leave that to the development of the case, but it would be 'conclusive and convincing to the twelve brilliant and incorruptible and intelligent gentlemen that he saw before him,' etc., etc. The counsel then proved several things which tended to weaken the case of the people considerably. They were, first: the servant-girl mentioned was 'sweet,' as a witness put it, on the hostler who had testified to hearing the threats of the prisoner, and her feelings were decidedly the reverse towards the accused; also that the hostler was a man of bad character by the records of the criminal court, and that Mari, when he discovered the wounded man, was returning from the city, which he had left, according to his testimony, five miles distant at about the time when, according to the people's witnesses, the wounds were probably inflicted. The lawyer then called my clerk and asked him if he had repeated aloud the answers of the dying man. No, he hadn't. Was he confident that the paper he read from was in the exact condition in which it was, when he delivered it to the coroner? He said, it was with the exception of the indorsement. He was also questioned as to whether he had noticed me when I made the indorsement, whether I wrote it on the left-hand side of the paper as handed me, or on the right-hand side? He said he had not. The slip of paper was then handed to the prisoner's counsel, who took a large envelope, cut a square hole in it, which, when the paper was placed in it, allowed nothing to be seen but the notes. After calling the attention of the court to this as an exhibit in the case, he said to the clerk : "I observe, sir, that there are spaces or gaps interpersed among the characters which represent the period at the end of the answers, or indicate that the answers or questions are indented or paragraphed?'

The witness acquiesced.

'That is to say,' the counsel went on, 'each answer or question in your notes is either 'indented' with a space at the beginning, or the space at the termination indicates the period— the blank means either the termination or beginning of the question or answer as the case may be ?'

The witness answered in the affirmative.

'Now, sir,' said the counsel, 'I will read the first question from the coroner's slip, and you give me the answer as it appears on your notes, with that side of the paper up.'

The lawyer here indicated to the witness the end of the paper he was to read from, which, as it turned out, was the opposite way from that in which the clerk had held it in making his previous transcript. He then read the question in this manner, the clerk giving the appended answers :"

1. " Could you identify the man, or give the authorities any information as to his character ?"

A. " Impossible—impossible to ; face covered ; could not."

2. "Was he there alone, or were there more than one ? "

A. "This man don't mean."

3. " Was the motive robbery ? "

A. " Robbery, think it was."

4. " Was the instrument used a knife ? "

A. " Yes, sir."

5. " Are you positive that this was one of them ? "

A. " Mistake—wrong man, sure."

6. " Was this man one of your assailants—can you identify him by his talk ?"

A. " At this talk, no ; I doubt him ; I am not sure."

7. " Can you give any account of the assault, or state what you did, or said, when you were attacked ? "

A. " No can tell ; no talk at all."

" That is the way the remarkable record was twisted and reversed.

There was a curious buzz in the court room. My clerk wilted as he faltered on with the answers, and I was thunderstruck. It was so long since the answers had been given, that perhaps the clerk knew but little about it—all he had to rely on was the notes. The clever lawyer had found out that they were two-edged and double-barrelled; they read upside down, or downside up, turned one way, one thing, another way, another thing, and then I was aware, for the first time, that my clerk was "rattled" the very instant that he had undertaken to transcribe the wretched marks, three days before. You see, I had been so anxious to play detective that I paid no attention to what the injured party said. Well, of course, the prisoner was acquitted, and the notes went to protest. Marks that could be read upside down, or down-side up, forward, or backward, etc., were not considered of much value, and, of course, the accused was acquitted. The jury never left their seats.

To conclude with, I will tell you this in confidence : The coroner who took that inquest has learned a thing or two. When he is a coroner, he proposes to act as a coroner, and not as a detective. And when he takes an ante-mortem statement he takes it himself, and he repeats the answers as given, and writes them in good, large, round, United States. That's all. I may add, that if Mari was not guilty in that case, the real culprit was never discovered. I always suspected him."

" What became of the clerk ? " said Mr. Northcoate.

"Oh!" answered the Coroner, musingly, "we parted, and he was employed afterwards driving mules on the Second avenue cars. Subsequently, I think, he went West, became secretary, and afterwards president of the Migginsville Railroad ; the last I heard of him was that he had been shot through the skull in some difficulty in Montana. I was quite sorry that I didn't hold the inquest ; it was a treat I had hoped for for some years."

"Well," said Mr. Northcoate, " it was time for him to die, but I never thought he would be shot through the head on account of the thick-ness——"

The Coroner interrupted : "Indeed, I think a man who could write notes that would be legible both ways, would be of inestimable value to some of the gentry in your profession, who have great difficulty in reading them *one way.*"

Just then the servant brought in coal to replenish the grate, and silently left the room.

The Coroner remarked thoughtfully ; " I know that face. Where have I seen that man ? Who is he ?"

"That," said the host, as he winked at the others, "that is an Italian : his name is John Simonetti."

The Coroner got up, looked hard at the company, and said, in an altered tone, " Good-night, gentlemen, good-night."

CHAPTER III.

THE STENOGRAPHER'S STORY.

THE meeting of the Worshipers at the Shrine was duly opened by the Host. "Tell us a story," he said to the Coroner, "to pass the time." "No, siree" was the emphatic answer; "you discredited my narrative of the clerk's notes which was just as true as that we sit here and sought to impugn "——

"Not at all," interrupted the Scribe, "I believe it implicitly. In fact I have known of far more remarkable things in my short and short hand career. Your tale was of notes that read either side up. What say you of notes that could not be read at all?"

"That," said the Coroner, "I know to be common; and when I hear fellows of your craft preferring the makeshift skeleton of short hand notes to double leaded newspaper print for legibility, I always think of Ananias." The others murmured assent. "To show you," resumed the Stenographer, "that I never in the least doubted the truth of your story, I will relate something even more singular. Your narrative was of double meaning notes that read downside up or upside down; what do you say to notes that could be read not only upside down and down side up, but inside out?"

"Indeed!" remarked the Taciturn Member. The other listeners looked at each other aghast.

"Give us the instance," said the Lawyer, in a

tone of unfeigned agitation, as with a great effort
he recovered himself sufficiently to wipe the cold
beads of perspiration from his wrinkled brow,
" and we will tell you what we think."

" By all means" broke in the Coroner, " anything to convince a 'Doubting Thomas,' and he
looked squarely at the Host. " There was once
a wall-eyed tom-cat," he went on, " that saw what
appeared to be a bull-dog's tail sticking out of a
thicket. Not fully satisfied by the evidence, he
went to investigate, and never doubted again.
His end was like that of the early martyrs."

" How ? " queried the lawyer.

"Why," remarked the little Coroner, as he
nodded triumphantly toward the sarcastic gentleman, " the 'doubting Thomas' died in faith.'

" I have the screed in my pocket," said the
Stenographer, ignoring the crest-fallen air of the
Host. " It was written by a young friend of
mine who was then employed on a daily paper.
After this manuscript was submitted to the editor, my friend was cashiered on the spot, as a
man not possessing sufficient veracity to meet
the requirements of one holding the position of
a newspaper reporter."

A chorus of " Oh's" greeted this statement.

The cold-blooded stenographer then produced
a roll of paper, and having straightened out the
folds and dog-eared the corners, began the reading of the singular narrative called :

THE FANLIGHT NOTES.

Miss Kitty Hammond was a picture as she sat
at her desk late that Saturday afternoon. She
was not biting her pencil in vain ; although a
native of Pennsylvania, she was a stenographer

or a stenographeress.   You could see that by the small black spot of smut on the left side of her nose.   This young lady was employed in the office of Mr. Theodore Moffet, the rich lawyer. They were not yet married, much as that gold-spectacled and eminently respectable looking gentleman would have liked to enter into the contract.   Hence, *he* was in the habit of dictating to *her*.

The girl who sat there was, as before stated, a picture, and quite a pleasant one at that, black spot and all.

She had a mouth too sweet for pencil moistening, a fair complexion, a soft blue eye—in fact two of them, hair just the right shade (golden-brown, as a description, is fair to middling for one who knows little about colors) and a nose—gracious ! one of those saucy, slightly turned—no, a great poet says " Tip-tilted like the petals of a flower." Further description is useless. You young fellows can think of one girl who is all perfection, sweeter and fairer than all others, and Miss Hammond was just that kind of a girl. Her father was a rather obscure and somewhat obstinate clergyman of the Methodist persuasion in the Town of ———. The reverend gentleman and the lawyer were old friends. Indeed, it was through the latter's financial standing and influence that the clergyman was placed over the Church of———.

These "Old Cronies" had several ideas in common ; and lately they had taken it into their venerable heads that a certain arrangement in which the rector's daughter was to be matrimonially disposed of, would be mutually satisfactory.

Although close-fisted, cross and domineering, Moffet was a respected, prospering lawyer ; and Mr. Hammond, blinded by love for his only daughter, and a paternal desire to see her well settled in life, was not unwilling that his old friend and benefactor should have every opportunity to make a matrimonial alliance with his daughter ; hence, he fell in with the lawyer's ideas at the first hint from that gentleman.   At her father's suggestion, the girl entered the employment of the attorney, "to earn pin-money," he said, although she scarcely needed it, for her father had been saving souls and money like a man in real earnest.   The "pin-money" excuse had a deep ulterior design known to both gentlemen, but not as yet fathomed by the young lady.

Moffet, as a prominent lawyer, was in the habit of bringing suits, and, of course, while in his employ he had the opportunity to press his own suit with the girl, and, indeed, he managed to make himself quite agreeable.

Miss Kitty, actuated by that spirit of independence born in most women and some men, accepted the employment gladly, but, as has been said, had not yet fallen in with the deep laid plan of the rector and the lawyer.

There was an obstacle in the way, that, if it did not blind her otherwise keen perception, certainly interfered seriously with her father's programme; for a young fellow, Thomas M. Offet by name, employed in the N. G. R. R. Co.'s office, was becoming interested in the young woman. He had as yet never told his love, but was only awaiting the "raise" which comes so early, often and suddenly to clerks in railroad offices, especially stenographic clerks, to put in a bid for that type-writer; and, being a very determined young stenographer, he meant to have that girl by hook or by crook.

Several times of late, young Offet had called at the office for Miss Hammond, and accompanied her home. Moffet discovering this endeavored to put a stop to these meetings by detaining his amanuensis in the evening at the office on one pretext or another, and occasionally escorted the young woman to her father's door himself.

Once or twice the young man visited Miss Hammond at her residence, but her father was always present during the evenings, and gave the young man no encouragement to call again. In fact, the reverend gentleman seemed to be consulting his repeater most of the time during

these visits, and managed to sit the young man
out.

Matters had been going on thus for some
time. The clergyman learned from Moffet that
young Offet had been calling at the office to see
the girl, and was not pleased thereat. As usual,
in such cases, made and provided, he made
things worse by a little foolish opposition.
" Do not allow that 'whipper-snapper,'" the
doctor called him, " near you, my child, he is
quite unfit company for you," and concluded
with some general remarks about the impecuni-
osity and general good-for-nothingness of the
young man. Miss Hammond did not draw
herself up to her full height, her eyes flashing
scorn, etc., as all young ladies do in novels under
like circumstances. This girl's height was just
four feet, eleven inches and a half, and the sublime and crushing effect would have been
entirely lost, so she did just what girls of that
age always do in similar circumstances,—took
the part of the abused party through pity ; and
" Pity is akin to love ; or is the Irishman's
quotation more truthful, " Achin' to love ?" At
all events the clergyman thought the girl could
not be so foolish as to stand in the way of a
good offer such as Moffet was sure, sooner or
later, to make ; and, while he acted as home
guard, he believed the lawyer would bring
matters to the happy and successful issue he
desired. Keeping a keen eye on his daughter
while she was at home, he escorted her to various
places, when Moffet was not on hand to perform
that agreeable duty, and fondly believed that
with his own espionage and Moffet's watchful-

ness, there could be no attachment nor any opportunity for the young man to prosecute his suit.

There had been, so far at least, between the girl and young Offet, nothing warmer than a budding friendship, which would never perhaps have ripened into anything stronger, but for the parental opposition.   They were interested in each other, but, as yet, nothing further.

Running Errands.

Now the office of Moffet was blessed, or cursed, with a boy—and such a boy. His name was Mike—just plain Mike, but his companions, as he said himself, "sometimes call me Moriarity for short."   The son of poor, but Irish parents, he was like all 14 year old boys, much deeper than he seemed to be. He kept both eyes and ears wide open, and to his limited ability was quick at everything but errands.

This lad was apparently respectful to his

employer, whom he both feared and disliked.
In Moffet's office, he was retained simply on
sufferance because he was useful and cheap.
Although earning but a few cents a day, his
employer exacted a petty fine if he delayed
in opening the office in the morning, or
spent too much time at lunch ; and the lad's
weakly pittance was often reduced by fines
and penalties which were rigorously exacted.
No wonder there was no love lost between
master and servant.   While he respectfully
"sir-red" his employer to his face, Mike sometimes so far forgot himself as to refer to the
lawyer as "the Old One," and by way of variety,
"His Nibs."   But these expressions were made
use of in out-of-the-way places, and in low
tones.

Miss Hammond's office was a little room separated from the main office (Moffet's) by a short
ground-glass partition and door that Michael
called her "Bow-door."

To enter her room the visitor passed from the
outer or main corridor through Moffet's office,
the main entrance to which was marked "Private."

The room in which the boy was employed was
entered from another corridor or hall on the left
or long side of the "L."   Between that room
and the lawyer's private office was still another
door, generally kept closed by Moffet's expressed wish, over which was the ordinary swing-
ing fanlight.   In this ante-room the boy was
accustomed to sit except when running, or perhaps we should say crawling errands.   It was a
standing rule in the office that the boy should

not enter the main or private office till sum-
moned by his employer. This was one of the
rules he strictly obeyed.   There seemed to be
an air of cleanliness, quietness and restraint
about the inner office that .was not to his taste.
Once or twice when in close proximity to his
employer he noticed a look of displeasure on his
face and a dangerous glitter in the elderly gentleman's eye that frightened him, and he rightly
attributed the look of disgust to the odor of a
cigarette which he had lately left half smoked
and still lighted on a window-sill on the outer
corridor.

This left corridor, as already said, was only
used by the boy in entering his room, and by
those having business with Moffet not of a private character. Persons who had not the entree
to the private office at the front hall went around
into the room occupied by the boy, who took the
visitor's card or wrote the name on a slip of
paper, as the case might be, and passed it
through an oblong slit in the door separating
the ante-room from the private office. Mike
preferred and enjoyed the freedom of the ante-
room where he reigned supreme, and where with
an occasional dab at a short hand book or keen
enjoyment of "The Stolen Maiden or the Red
Outlawed Indian's Bloody Hand" he managed
to pass the time pleasantly enough, when not engaged in throwing wads of wet paper through
the air-shaft at the boy down-stairs or stealing a
smoke in the silent corridor.

As already intimated, he was employed on
sufferance. Angry words with an occasional
muttered oath thrown at him, had not been un·

common, but of late the presence of Miss Hammond had served to curb exhibitions of Moffet's temper in her hearing at least, and for this, among other things, the lad was grateful to her. Much to the boy's disgust he was detained quite late on this particular Saturday evening. Mr. Tom M. Offet, between whom and the lad a lasting friendship had sprung up, called and had a long sit of it in the ante-room. Once the lawyer opened the door and speaking to the lad and at the visitor whom he recognized, roared : " Boy, do not allow us to be disturbed by any callers unless the business is of the utmost importance," and slammed the door to. " No use waiting," whispered the lad to Offet, " they're in there till they finish that brief or job, whatever it is." Notwithstanding the hint, the young man remained. An hour passed. Young Offet fidgeted in his chair and in many ways exhibited his impatience ; at length Michael approached the door ostensibly to light the gas when much to his surprise there was no response to his repeated knock. He turned the knob, the room was empty. "They're gone," he gasped ; " I guess they went off together, they often do now ; it's getting interesting." Then seeing the look of disappointment on the other's face he consolingly remarked : " I'll help you," and in a tragic, Old Bowery tone, " Fear not, I will rescue her or die." The dreadful alternative was lost on the ears of the young man as with a crestfallen air he passed from the corridor down into the street. He comforted himself with the reflection that the young woman was not aware that he had been in waiting in the ante-room when she left the office with her elderly escort. Nor was he far wrong in this supposition. As for Mike he kicked over the waste-basket, banged the windows down with a rush and was about to insert the key in the door when he saw an oblong piece of paper projecting from the pocket of Mr. Moffet's office-coat, which hung on the door frame.

He was a boy ; his mother was a woman, and perchance he is not to be too severely condemned for the possession of a curiosity that prompted him to open that paper.

He spread it out as he neared the window, the better to see it in the gathering dusk. What he saw made him exclaim almost involuntarily: " By Jimmenaddy ! " It was a marriage license issued by the County Clerk of a neighboring county, addressed to "any justice of the peace in and for," &c., "duly authorized to solemnize marriage," and "This day appeared before me, Theo. Moffet, one of the contracting parties, of the town of ——, and Richard Hammond, father and natural guardian of Kate Hammond, the aforementioned party, residents of," &c. It was plentifully interspersed with whereases and hereinbefores, &c.

The boy blew a long, low whistle. His curiosity satisfied, he was about to return the paper to the place it came from, but in folding it up he saw something that surprised him. As he had held the upper part of the document in a position to read, the lower portion naturally rested on the lighted end of the half consumed cigarette between his fingers, and a little circular brown spot showed in the paper just below the County

Clerk's signature. He wet his finger and attempted to rub the stain off. The result frightened him. The charred spots fell out and
a small round hole appeared with dark ser-
rated edges. Then all thought of replacing
the paper was abandoned. It would bear
the marks of having been handled, he
thought ; an investigation would in all probability lead to his prompt dismissal if not
to some other great punishment. He thought
of his mother—she was a widow and he was her
only son, and the pittance he received, small as
it was, helped to pay the rent. It would not do
to lose it. He would destroy the paper and say
nothing. It would never be found out. The
very fact of Moffet's having left it in the pocket
of his office coat showed that he was careless and
would in reality never know what had become of
it. He would make away with it, get a duplicate copy, or do something ; and as he hesitated,
and thought of all this he almost unconsciously
slipped the paper in his pocket intending to
think out carefully what was best to be done in
the matter. His next impulse was to see Miss
Hammond and tell her all. But how could he
face her and admit that he had purloined it. It
was hardly a thing to be proud of ; she had been
kind to him in many ways, and he desired to retain her good opinion. At length the impression
became strong in the lad's mind that the girl
was entirely in the dark as to the arrangement
hinted at in the paper. If he could warn her of
the secret plan and also save himself from any
evil consequences it would please him. If he
could not pluck up courage to tell her, he would

see young Offet and put the whole matter in his hands.

The more the boy thought over the matter the more he was convinced that there was a hidden design under consideration ; that he had discovered "a put up job," he called it, and the opportunity to interfere with a cherished plan of his ill-tempered old employer was not to be foregone. He even convinced himself, after much cogitation, that he was doing a good turn to his friends, Miss Hammond and Offet, in fact, a clever thing. He would, however, see the latter in the morning before business hours, and meantime he would sleep over it and see what the morrow's sun would bring forth.

Mike was a boy, and he slept the sleep of the just. At an early hour on the following day he called at the young man's residence. Offet had left some time before. The boy consoled himself with the reflection that he would see him in the course of the day. He retained the abstracted paper in his pocket, not having the courage to destroy it till he had shown it to some one.

How the long morning passed, he never knew. Once or twice he fancied he heard Moffet rumaging through the pigeon holes and about the desk, and trembled when called. The lawyer did not refer to his loss. Had he done so, there was an unmitigated lie ready for him. On his way to the post-office about midday, the lad managed to call and see Mr. Offet; the story was soon told and corroborated by the production of the license. To say that the lover was astonished would be putting it mildly. He was mad. "A despicable trick," he savagely exclaimed, "to trap the dear girl unwittingly. I am sure she is no party to it. I am surprised at her father and astounded at the audacity of that old villain." He conjectured that it was the father's intention to take the girl on a trip to some distant place where Moffet would join them, and then, remote from the influence of friends, including himself, the girl would be prevailed upon by her father and Moffet to go through the ceremony, of which the procuring of the license was the first step. He had no idea things had gone so far; he was much startled. Now there was no time to hesitate. Nothing but the great pressure of business in the office of the N. G. R. R. Co. (it was the time of the great "strike") prevented him from rushing at once to the lawyer's office and blowing up or cleaning out the whole concern. Offet felt that he must act promptly, because, with a license ready—and perhaps a duplicate copy of the one purloined was on its way, if not already procured—and the girl in a distant place under her father's control, what could prevent the complete success of the plot? Only the girl's will, and he feared this would give way under the united arguments of the doctor and the lawyer. He was in a quandary. He would write her a note at once, telling her he would call that evening; but perhaps her father's intention was to leave the city with her to-night, yet, a note of warning written promptly, seemed the only thing possible. "No," said the boy thoughtfully, as young Offet took his note book from his pocket; "it is useless to write, Moffet, I guess, would get it." "And I fear,"

said the other, "that her father receives her
letters at the house, and, I presume, reads them,
but he is her father; surely I can send her a
note to the office." "Well," said the boy, " I
don't see how it is to be delivered when it is
written; he watches her like a cat watching a
mouse. Perhaps I might find some way. Oh !
I have it ; write it in shorthand, and, if he does
get it, he will be none the wiser." "A good
idea," remarked Offet, tearing a leaf from his
note book, and jotting down a few sentences ;
" I shall send her this, and if, as you say, he is
mean enough to intercept it, he won't understand it, that's one comfort." " May I read it ?"
inquired the boy. " Certainly," answered the
other. " Because," the lad went on, " if it is lost
or intercepted I may have a chance to see her
and state its contents." " By all means," replied
the young man, " read it ; I will not wait to seal
it, it is not necessary." " Good, good," ejaculated the lad, " don't wait to enclose it. I'm
behind time now. I will try and get it to her
someway or other."

Mike took the hurriedly addressed note, and
after getting the mail at the post office, thought
it would save time, having reached Moffet's, to
let the elevator boy hand in the letters, while he
went to a curb-stone restaurant for a two-cent
dinner.

Having put himself outside of a large wedge
of Washington pie, and having regaled himself
with a cigarette, he at length concluded, before
re-entering the office, to fish out Offet's note to
Miss Hammond, so as to have it ready to hand
her if an opportunity presented itself. To his

intense surprise he failed to find it. Search as he would, in every receptacle about his clothing, he failed to discover it, and a look of dismay over-spread his face as he surmised that the elevator boy had received it among the other letters, and had handed all in to the lawyer. He dashed up-stairs, hoping almost against hope, that "Elevator" had not as yet delivered the letters. "Oh, yes," the latter said cheerfully, in answer to his eager inquiry, he had given them all into Mr. Moffet's own hand. No, he did not notice any unsealed note addressed to Miss Hammond, or a small red-lined sheet of note paper. It fact, he didn't look at any of the letters ; he never looked at letters or cards, or anything; no, never ; and if anyone thought he did such a thing, let them deliver their own letters.

The lad saw that there was nothing further to be gained by parleying and congratulated himself that as he knew what was in the note he could deliver a verbal message to the same effect or write another note just as good.

Having entered the ante-room he waited close to the inner door what seemed to him a long time to learn if the lawyer departed from the office or to discover if the girl left her seat. The outer door never opened. The steady clickity-click of the type-writer, and the lengthening shadows warned him that the afternoon was slipping by without the accomplishment of his purpose. He began to fidget, and at length concluded to write a note with the intention of getting it to the girl in some way. The communication ready in his hand he seemed to be no nearer the consummation of his purpose. It would not do to call her out to the front door, Moffet would see him, and to wait longer was out of the question. Then the idea occurred to him of dropping the note through the open fanlight over the door leading from the ante-room to the private office and trusting that the young lady would find it on the floor before Moffet saw it. It was a desperate chance and he would investigate first. It seemed practicable, and he thought it wise to endeavor to first attract her attention in some way. Taking a tall office stool he climbed upon it and was barely able to look into the room. Cautiously slipping down and getting a Webster's Unabridged, he placed it on the stool and as cautiously mounted again. Then he slowly and carefully unloosened the cord by means of which and a broom handle the sash was swung and lifted the fanlight out from the sockets in which its pivots rested. He laid the transom on the floor and mounting the perch, again looked in. The view was good. He saw Moffet just below the opening with his back towards the door, three or four law books in his lap and a large roll of legal cap in his hand. A few feet beyond sat Miss Hammond clicking away at the machine and occupying such a position that just the outer edge of her left ear was towards him, a pose known to photographers and football players as three-quarter back. The boy saw at once that owing to the respective positions of the parties, dropping the message through the opening without attracting the lawyer's attention was almost if not quite beyond the possibilities. He hoped she

might raise her eyes, and he stared at the girl
steadily for some minutes waving his hands in
the air, up and down, crosswise, lengthwise and
otherwise, in the vain effort to attract her attention without Moffet's knowledge. It was useless.
He even attempted to make a low hissing noise
between his teeth; it was barely audible to himself, and faint as it was frightened him.

Another scheme occurred to him : he would
make what school boys call a " spit-ball " and
throw it at her. This idea was dismissed as soon
as formed. He argued that if it were thrown so as
to strike her with sufficient force to serve his
purpose it would startle her, perhaps cause her
to utter an exclamation of some sort and then it
was all up.

All these thoughts passed through the lad's
mind in less time than t takes to relate the occurrence. Completely baffled, he descended
from his position to think, and just scratched
his head in sheer despair. After replacing the
book and stool a new idea entered his fertile
mind. Taking up a sheet of paper he made
several idiotic looking marks on it and held it to
the light. He was not satisfied. Again and
again he tried it and finally after holding the
paper between his face and the window he
chuckled softly. His glance fell on the displaced
transom and he grinned. With difficulty he suppressed a loud guffaw. "There is the fanlight,"
he muttered to himself, " here is a bottle of ink,
a mucilage brush and a stenographer; what's the
matter with that?"

Nothing. He took up the transom, laid it on
his knee and without waiting to clean the mu-

cilage from the brush, dipped it in the ink and wrote the message for Miss Hammond on the glass. Then cooly and cautiously he replaced the sash with its pinions in the sockets, quite

Trying it on

confident that in the course of the day the young lady would look up and see the message, and that even if Muffet observed it, he was outwitted.

CHAPTER IV.

THE FANLIGHT NOTES.—*Continued.*

AS Mike surveyed his work he laughed softly and shook hands with himself taking his left hand in his right and giving it the proper motion while repeating the immortal words of the great John Horner, "He put in his thumb, pulled out a plum saying, Oh! what a good boy am I."

As stated the transom swung on pivots. When the sash was not pushed or pulled to the perpendicular it swung to the horizontal, being pivoted in the end centers, and if swung half around the top of course became the bottom. When the cord attached to the upper end was pulled the sash fell to the horizontal—open—the top balancing the bottom; a position it was often kept in during warm weather. When in its proper place and closed recourse was had to the cord to pull or the stick to push as the case might be. Being of a mechanical turn of mind the lad noticed this when removing the sash and replaced it so that the message for the girl would appear properly. The reader paused : "I will show you what the writer intended to represent—a working model, made as well as could be with transparent paper. It explains it much better than any verbal description, but how it could be arranged to appear in a book or magazine in this satisfactory shape, I am at a loss to imagine."

" And in order to convince his readers of the truth of his narrative the writer, like Mr. Wegg, dropped into poetry."

" Ah," said the Host blandly, " that reminds me ; a person was once boasting of having killed a notorious burglar who attempted to rob him. His listeners did not seem to believe the statement. But the boaster in order to convince them of the truth of his assertion, produced a map and proudly pointed out on it the country in which the killing took place, as he said, to convince his hearers."

The others nodded, while the Stenographer went gloomily on :

" This, as I say, represents the door and the fanlight. It is in fact, as I have already told you, a working model. The descriptive poetry as you perceive, is written across the main panel of what represents the door. Observe the rope, the broom-handle and all with the lines.

> " This is the door that swung on the floor
>   With the pivoted fanlight above ;
> One turn of the sash, and quick as a flash,
>   In darted the God of Love.
>
> This is the string that moved the thing,
>   And this is the stick of like aid ;
> This is the cleat that held the rope neat,
>   And this is the sign that Mike made."

After the company had somewhat recovered and the Host and Engineer had called loudly for water, the unabashed Stenographer continued the reading : " As I was saying, he placed the transom bearing the short hand characters in such a position that the message for the girl would appear properly. Replacing it and tying the cord fastened to the sash on the cleat at the door-frame, the boy sat by his desk with teeth clenched tightly and almost choked in his effort to prevent himself from laughing. He sat there for some time with the glow of feeling that he had done a good day's work. Suddenly the office door opened with a bang against the wall, that shook the building, and the angry face of Moffet appeared. Glaring at the boy, he shouted : " Here, you ; send Biglore to me instantly, you rat ; tell him to come into my office by the private door. Do you hear? Go ! "

The boy's heart beat fast. Biglore, he knew, was a stenographer, having an office on the floor above. In fact, there were several of that calling in the building. They fell over each other in the passage-way and jostled each other on the stairs. Biglore was one of the best. The boy stole a timid glance at the hard face of his employer and needed no second bidding. Slowly he went up the stairs, his breath coming short and fast. " Will it work ? " he muttered. " Oh, it must not fail ! I have tried it ; it cannot fail. It is as solid as a rock, and they needn't think because I'm Irish, born in Jersey, that I don't know—" His cogitations were cut short by his arrival at Mr. Biglore's door. The message delivered to that gentleman, the boy turned quickly in an endeavor to hurry down. " I will accompany you," said Mr. Biglore, taking the unwilling boy's arm in his and meandering down the broad stairway to Moffet's office. " You are to go in by the private door," said Mike, shifting uneasily, " and mind you, sir, rub your feet well on that mat—rub them hard. He's awful particular, he is. Don't hurry yourself." Leaving Biglore industriously scraping his feet on the mat at the private entrance, Mike dashed around the corridor and into the ante-room. Quickly approaching the inner door, he unfastened the

As it appeared to Mike in his room when he set it for Biglore in Moffet's room.

end of the rope from the cleat, pulled it, and with the broomstick quietly pushed the lower part of the fanlight up. He believed that Moffet would meet Biglore at the outer private door, and surmised that he could go through the performance just related, unnoticed. Knowing that it was a desperate chance, he took it. He reasoned well. It succeeded. Scarce had he turned the transom and settled himself, when he heard the voices of Moffet and Biglore just below the opening.

"And I have reason to believe," the former was saying, "that my boy, or some other irresponsible person (he had Offet in mind) is taking a dishonorable, surreptitious, and underhand method of sending insulting, or at least impertinent communications to myself or to my lady amanuensis, and I have sent for you to read that, if you please." "What? Where is it?" inquired the dazed Biglore. "Those characters on the fanlight—that Chinese inscription ; read it, please, and translate it for me. Miss Hammond, you take this down as Mr. Biglore reads it."

The bewildered Biglore raised his eyes to the transom, scanned it carefully, and remarked, after a pause : "It does not seem to be very alarming, sir, so far as I can make it out. It is really the most heart-rending short hand I ever beheld, but I believe this is the reading—"

"Oh, read it, read it, read it !" exclaimed the lawyer, impatiently.

Mr. Biglore hemmed twice or thrice, paused and hesitated as he looked at the coarse characters slobbered by the careless boy with the gummy brush on the not over clean glass.

He then read and Miss Hammond made the transcript as follows :
"Oh, Doctor K.

"How can a fish have meat by mistake? Color it. For it will save all year for each of two, if not more. Give the vile dust. Sell the sinner. Although the officials may say what? Get off the perch.

"But don't go."

As it appeared to Biglore in Moffet's room after Mike set the trap in the ante-room.

"It may be nonsense," concluded Biglore, "Perhaps a cipher or secret code, but I doubt that, though I have heard of such things. In all probability it is as I have read it, substantially." "Is that all?" queried the dumbfounded lawyer.

"All, sir, and I think it is perfectly harmless unless you have reason to think otherwise."

"Humph," muttered the counselor, "I suspected that it might have been something much more serious than that." He glanced furtively in the waste paper basket and noticed that certain pieces of red-lined note paper were much too small to be pieced without great difficulty, and he regretted now that he had not saved that sheet for a translation.

" It must be as you say, and if so, it is without meaning. You are quite confident that is a correct translation?"

"Oh, certainly," answered Mr. Biglore, "I believe it to be substantially so," turning to Miss Hammond who nodded her head in the affirmative.

" Well," said the lawyer, following the stenographer to the private door, "I am obliged to you and I am glad that it is as harmless and nonsensical as you say, because—"

" Oh, by the way," interrupted Biglore, as he stood in the hallway, " let us have a glance at it on the other side."

" Of course, if you desire," answered the lawyer, and both turned the corridor leading to the ante-room.

" Mike, Mike," said a suppressed voice through the key-hole, " they have gone around."

Mike heard the voice and in the twinkling of an eye had the string pulled with such a jerk that it broke from the ring in the sash, the fanlight opened and reversed with the broomhandle, and his mouth demurely set by the time the stenographer and Moffet entered the ante-room.

Mr. Biglore glanced at the inverted sash and with a very perplexed look scratched his left ear. The lawyer and stenographer saw at a glance that without a string attached to the sash it could not be turned without difficulty. .Then

As it appeared to Biglore in Mike's room after he and the sash had " gone round."

Biglore's face brightened. " Never mind," he said, "you must excuse me, sir, but in reading short hand notes position is everything, and as this is reversed to me I perceive I shall have to accommodate myself to circumstances and re-

verse myself as it were." Saying this the stenographer turned his back to the fanlight door,
raised his coat tails carefully and lowered his
head so that he could get a view between his
nether extremities. He seemed to be making
an impossible attempt to stand on his head while
keeping on his feet. His position was undignified and ridiculous—perhaps better imagined
than described—suffice it to say the pose was
such that nothing but the presence of his employer restrained Mike from shouting "Spurrins!
Stick in your noddle," and taking a frog-like
leap over the arched back of Biglore and finishing with the boyish yell of " P-a-r-r ! "

All this time the lad sat with his chair tilted
back against the wall, his hands nervously
twisting the end of his soft hat, the rest of which
was in his mouth ; his knees working up and
down convulsively and from his bulging eyes
and red distorted face he appeared to be suffering all the dreadful agonies of a violent epileptic
fit or the final spasms of hydrophobia.

In the curious manner described the accommo-
dating stenographer scanned the boy's coarse inscription, and naturally proceeded to read it
from left to right and from the top down as he
viewed it. In reality he began at the lower
right-hand corner and read to the left upwards
as anyone would who took his odd position and
began from the bottom.

The stenographer thanked his stars that Miss
Hammond could not see him for he felt that his
position was anything but dignified and whether
from a feeling of gentlemanly modesty which
all stenographers possess, or from his singularily

unnatural position he flushed to his collar bone.

Not long did he remain in his dreadful pose but while he was thus standing on his head as it were, trying to decipher the fanlight inscription

"One good turn deserves another."—Reading the fanlight notes in Mike's room.

Miss Hammond stood at lady-like ease in the other room looking at the message.

"It is the same here," said Biglore, thoughtfully, as his face resumed its natural color, "it is all right, of course ; it ought to be,"

"Of course," echoed the lawyer, in a matter-of-fact tone, "how could it be otherwise?"

"It could not," murmured Biglore as he slow-ly left the room with Moffet, "of course not."

Ah, it could be otherwise, it was otherwise, and the office boy knew it, and by this time Miss Hammond certainly knew it, for while the others were going around Mike's voice went through the keyhole, singing :

"Hail Columbia, Right side up side."

By the pulling of a string, it read as Biglore indicated, and by the poke of a broom-handle it was :

"Oh, Dear K.

"Although the lover's note was read, good will and patience.   Look out for yourself ; you, your pa, and the old one go to N. Y. State, Illinois or West.

"I gave the lawyer your note.   Ransack, grab it.

"But don't go."

For the first time Miss Hammond looked up, for the first time she saw the message. A quick-witted girl, with a glance or two and a little study she comprehended it. A trip with her father and Moffet to a distant State ? Why ? It was a revelation to her. The idea ! A note to her ! What is that ? And suppressed ? Moffet gave her no note. "Ransack ?" Where ? Had he witheld it ? Could it be possible that such a thing had been done by this polite old gentle-man? That was the meaning of the fanlight message. She could hardly credit it, yet, what object had this boy in writing such a communi-cation in such a singular manner and at such risks to himself, if it were not the fact? She began to think seriously and little acts and circumstances came to her mind that had been almost forgotten; such as Moffet's escorting her home so frequently; the fact that young Offet had

As it appeared to Miss Hammond in Moffet's room when she read it at lady-like ease.

called to visit her once or twice previously, as she had reason to believe from a hint dropped by her father when she was not aware of that fact; the lawyer's request that she should delay her departure from the office on the pretended ex-

cuse of work to be done which she had suspected and subsequently discovered was only a pre-
tense, and a certain conversation that she had
with young Offet at Aunt Benson's house several
evenings before and a promise, a conditional
one to be sure, but a sweet one nevertheless;
the parting at the gate and—and a hint of letters
she had failed to receive, coupled with the young
man's evident desire to screen her father; all—
all came back to her. The girl's mind was in a
whirl. She would just take a walk and think it
over, and without a word to her employer she
whisked out. Mike heard the vexed girl slam
the outer door and hastened in to find Moffet
reading a brief or pretending to and wondering if
the angry girl suspected anything. "Did you
call me, sir," inquired the boy? "No, leave me
at once, sir. When I call you, you will know it
go to the post-office and hurry back."

The agitated girl had not yet reached the corner as, with a laugh and a skip, Mike approached
her. "Oh, didn't we play him," he began.
"Listen to me," she said, her face pale with in-
dignation, "did he get a note for me and keep
it?"

The boy related the circumstances of handing
the mail to the elevator man and his strong suspicion that her note from Offet was among the
letters that had reached Moffet's hands. She remembered then that she had seen him with a
sheet of red-lined note paper which he tore in
small bits as he eyed her curiously. She thought
it queer at the time, but now the inference was
plain. And the license the boy told her of, so
suspiciously procured, showing that they in-

tended to marry her off-hand without consulting
her wishes. "Oh, they did, indeed!" She
would see about that. Nothing but vexation
kept her from bursting into tears. As it was she
was in a fine state of temper. "The old villain!
the wretch!" she ejaculated, "to accompany
me home while playing such tricks. Gracious
me, I shall never step foot another day in his
office. The tricky old scamp!" Mike's efforts
as a pacifier were not of the best; he was a boy,
and did not understand young ladies in tan-
trums, but he suddenly ceased his poor efforts
as he cried : "Hi, there," and young Offet came
towards them.

The latter saw by the girl's face that there was
something amiss, and calling a cab he handed
her in, and directed the Jehu to drive to the park.
Before they started, the lad asked him to promise
faithfully to stop at Aunt Benson's on their return. "Do" he said, "looking earnestly at Offet,
the game is yours if you only go in and win, the
plan can be arranged."

Now, I forgot to tell you that Offet had received that "raise" and all he needed to make
his happiness complete was the consent of a
young woman about the size of Miss Hammond.
He was under the impression that once the knot
was properly tied there would be the usual for-
giveness from the father, and he tried earnestly
to convince the girl of that fact. Forgetful of
the promise he had made himself, to spare the
old man for the daughter's sake, he plumply
told her of communications sent her which she
had never received, of numerous occasions when
he waited in the ante-room to escort her only

to find that she had left with Moffet, and intimated that there was a scheme of the lawyer's
on foot, whose influence with her father she
well knew, to entrap her into a hasty marriage.

He soon learned from her that she had indig-
nantly left the lawyer's employ, and was disin-
clined to see her father just yet, until she had
recovered her composure, or—temper. The
time seemed propititous and the young man
ardently pressed his suit. He spoke eloquently
of his love, his brightening prospects, the comfortable home he had with only a younger sister
to keep house. "Dear Kitty," he urged, "we
have been kept apart by circumstances we could
not control ; we are together now ; I offer you
my home, my life, my protection—I love you."

The girl covered her face with her hands,
sobbing, "I am friendless and alone, a conspiracy against me, even my own father"——

"Kitty," the impassioned lover whispered,
"you have me to love and protect you forever,
be mine, come and we will end all this wretched
trouble at once. Come, love."

The woman hesitated, and the woman that
hesitates is won. "It seems so foolish," she
piteously exclaimed through her tears ; "so
sudden, without preparation, and my father"—
then she broke down utterly at the remem-
brance of her condition, believing that her own
father was in a plot to dispose of her like a
chattel. The suppressed letters, the many ful-
some and disgusting attentions of Moffet came
to her recollection and her opposition weakened.
The young man earnestly endeavored to prove
that now was the accepted time, that there was

nothing half so sweet in life as Love's young
dream, and paused only when he believed that
the day was won and with it the girl.

He deeply regretted now the lateness of the
hour as it would necessitate waiting another day
for the issuing of a marriage license. A delay
however short was dangerous. This girl might
change her mind if she reached home and were
again under her father's control, no matter how
great her love for him. A postponement might
result disastrously to his hopes, but there seemed
to be no help for it.

Miss Hammond, as a discreet young woman,
finally consented to go to her aunt's house, consult that good lady, and abide by her decision.

The Mrs. Benson, to whose home they went
was a life-long friend of Mike's mother, and
was, moreover, well acquainted with Offet and
his family, therefore a mutual friend, and in the
present crisis as the sequel showed, a friend indeed. A matter-of-fact woman of the world,
with a woman's quick perception she knew the
situation of affairs at a glance. She welcomed
the young couple with unusual warmth, embraced
her niece affectionately, and congratulated the
young fellow on his success in "hurrying the
thing up." "Oh, you rogue," she said smilingly,
"you need not look so innocently surprised.
Squire —— sent word that he would be on
duty at 7.30 and that it was all right, and as you
have set your hearts on it, and every one is
willing, I don't see what's the use of waiting.
When John and me got ready, we didn't wait a
minute either. Yes, you silly goose," she
whispered to the blushing girl, "at once, and I
will go along."

CHAPTER V.

THE FANLIGHT NOTES.—*Continued.*

NOW all this put young Offet in a singular condition of mind.   The good lady spoke as if
something were arranged and the Squire ready.
Ready for what?   He could not understand it,
yet there was a handsome girl beaming on him,
he loved her, she had tacitly consented to be his,
her aunt was there to chaperone her, anxious, it
seemed, that the "felicity should eventuate."
How did it come about?   Had the father, hearing of his promotion, withdrawn his opposition?
Perhaps the doctor's name had been forged to
the license and he had repudiated the proposed
alliance with Moffet.   The extraordinary turn of
affairs was incomprehensible to the young man;
the girl was in a fair way to become Mrs. Offet,
and he believed he could nerve himself up to
stand the consequences.

Mrs. Benson, with smiles and winks, conducted them to Squire ———'s, hard by, where that
legal riveter was awaiting them.   Ordinarily
that alone should have startled Offet, but he
was in such a delightfully dazed condition, the
victim of a good-natured conspiracy as it were,
that had the old gentleman himself suddenly
appeared and presented him with a check for
$10,000 he would have taken it as a matter of
course.

The parties being placed by Mrs. Benson,
the Squire asked the groom if he was Thomas
M. Offet and if the bride was Miss Kate Hammond, both residents of ———.   The answers

being in the affirmative, the knot was promptly
and effectually tied. The squire then laid down
the papers and took off his glasses the better to
kiss the bride. As he made his accustomed
jump the alert young lady stooped to imprint a
chaste salute on the brow of Michael, who appeared from no one knew where. The old
gentleman missed the bride but managed to give
Tom Offet a hearty smack on the left ear. The
young man turned to rub the injured member,
and then and for the first time got a good glance
at the paper which the squire had placed on a
chair. Lo ! It had a small round hole below the
Clerk's signature, and " Theo. M offet " was
easily mistaken by the near-sighted old man for
" Thos. M. Offet," especially as he had been applied to previously on behalf of certain parties
and had written the names of the bride and
groom in his own large plain characters.

Young Offet saw it all now, and I can hardly
describe his feelings of mingled consternation
and delight. He began to consider in a vague
way the consequences and at first concluded to
say nothing. On the whole, why should he.
Why not take the gifts the gods send ? It was
a wretched misunderstanding on their part, yet
he was not at fault, and it could not be helped
now. No, it was too late in any event, and, if
silence was not golden in this case it was the
least of two evils and therefore preferable. The
blushing bride, receiving the congratulations of
her aunt and the squire's wife seemed to be
happy, and was he to blurt out the truth and
cloud her fair face ? He saw now that the boy
had engineered the whole thing and by means

of the purloined license. It had been shown to the aunt and the squire, and they had been grossly deceived.

The poor girl, of course, had never been married before, and supposed having her aunt by her side, her father's sister (she having been motherless for many years) that everything was straightforward and proper.

Then the young man began to think of the disagreeable results when the facts came out and he bitterly blamed the boy; yet, there was his young wife, the tears of happiness streaming down her face; she was his, and as he looked at her he really thought the end justified the means.

Intending to seize Mike and make him confess the whole thing he looked about for him. The boy was gone. That resource having failed him he finally concluded to tell Mrs. Benson the facts at once and fully and be guided by her. Offet was not the man to take advantage of a misunderstanding for any reason, or to place himself in a false position, and after some difficulty he put the aunt in possession of all his facts and suspicions.

To his great surprise, the good lady, who had no sympathy for Moffet, looked on the whole thing as providential and concluded that it was all for the best. She was even pleased that her eyes were not as sharp as they had been twenty years ago and concluded by saying that perhaps, after all, the boy was not so much to blame.

"All's well that ends well." Through the intercession of Aunt Benson, Dr. Hammond was

appeased, and when, at the wedding breakfast a
few days after the marriage he became affection-
ate and mellow " with much drinking of wine,"
and murmured "Bless you, my children" the
irrepressible Mike was on hand and despite a
mouthful of good things, responded with quite a
solemn Amen. And Tom Offet and his bloom-
ing young wife and even the clergyman forgave
him for the trick about the license because of
his cleverness in making "THE FANLIGHT
NOTES."

The Stenographer ceased reading and folded
up the paper amid profound silence.

"Is that all" said the Engineer in a voice of
deep disappointment.

"What more do you want" answered the narrator in an injured tone.

"Well, I. supposed" the other went on, looking at the company "that that Offet fellow
would have got the Mike boy into the railroad
company's employ and that he would be now
Secretary of the Company if not President or
Treasurer. Don't it say so ?"

" No," said the Stenographer calmly, tying up
the manuscript and placing it in his pocket, " he
is still with Counsellor Moffet as managing clerk
and receives the munificent salary of $9 a
week."

" Ah," remarked the Host, "it reads like an
able lie, but of course, it isn't. What a great
pity that he was left an orphan at such an early
age, that his father died so young."

" How so ?" queried the Coroner.

" I am morally certain," murmured the Host,
" that your late clerk was that boy's father."

The meeting adjourned in great disorder.

CHAPTER VI.

THE DEAD MAN'S NOTES.—THE ENGINEER'S STORY.

THE parties met pursuant to adjournment. Present, the Host, the Coroner, Engineer Whitcomb, the Stenographer, the Lawyer and the Real Estate man.

The proceedings were opened by the remark from the Host, " Now, then," addressed to the Engineer.

The latter shifted uneasily in his seat, moved his left foot over his right, and after a moment's thought began :

"I am afraid, gentlemen, that you have slowed up at the wrong station. I might open the throttle and give you a straight run, concerning an odd instance about the rail for I, in common with others in a business supposed to be extremely hazardous, but which in reality is only exciting and enticing—have met with some curious events in my time. But it appears to me that you expect something upon the subject of stenography, and though I have made many dangerous curves, straight dashes, have been behind time, got off the track and made full stops as often as anyone, yet short hand is a subject of which I know very little and about which I care less. Notwithstanding this, I think to-night I am in a position to run off a short and quite interesting incident, but I do so under dispatchers' orders, and, at second hand.

"Some years ago I ran the special between

Montery and Philippsburgh on the G. O. P. As
my real tour of duty did not commence till we
reached the latter place I often whiled away the
thirty minutes' run when I was not with the engineer or in the caboose, in the mail-car, watching Tom Mulligan, the mail clerk, as he sorted
the letters.   Tom was a very decent fellow and
a man in many respects after my own heart.   In
order to understand my feelings towards Mulligan, I should say first that there was a dashing
young widow with an equally dashing daughter
who kept the hotel known as the ' Train Men's
Retreat,' a very respectable and well conducted
hotel at Philippsburgh, much frequented by
railroad men.   It was before Tom married the
daughter, and I was keeping company with the
widow. I supposed at the time that he was making up to the widow, and he believed I was
throwing sheep's eyes at the daughter, and of
course, there was hot rivalry between us and
some feeling in consequence; but when he slipped
out one night with the daughter, got coupled and
returned in time to have an understanding with
me and to tell me 'to go in and win,' and that
he would use his influence with the mother in
my behalf, we clasped hands and from being
rivals became fast friends, and have remained so
to this day.

"Mulligan left the position of mail agent, very
suddenly, to accept something better, just before he married this girl, as I have stated, and
he is now a rising man in Chicago."

" How about the widow ?" said the Host
softly.

" Somehow," answered the Engineer with a

sigh, " I did not ' ketch on, ' although it was not
Mull.'s fault.   It was the widow herself.   The
late lamented had been on the road and she was
afraid of train men, she said.   He was like that
fellow that lost the fight last week."   .

"How so?" inquired the Host.

·" He was over-trained," answered the Engineer with another deep sigh,` "fell under it,
running ' wild cat.' "

The Host seemed to be much interested in
the door-frame at which he gazed steadily under
the pitying glances of the others.

The Engineer resumed :   " While we were
keeping company—I think it was one Sunday
night, the widow had been singing the old hymn
' Shall we know each other there,' that brought
up the subject of whether people follow their
earthly vocations in the other world, and she
wondered if her ' dear Harry ' was still an engineer.   So I in joke suggested perhaps he was a
fireman, and do you know she afterwards sent
me a note about her fear of engineers, quoting
Bludso, ' them engineers is all purty much
alike,' etc., and that I was so fond of joking, I
might ' brake ' her heart, etc., and the thing fell
through."   The Engineer sighed deeply several
times and after a pause went on :

"Mull. was a trump.   Without doubt he was
the most truthful man I have ever known, except perhaps, you two gentlemen" (here the Engineer laid his hand on his left breast and
bowed politely in the direction of the Coroner
and the Stenographer.   The salute was returned
with great dignity by the individuals referred to).

"Before Mull.'s departure for the West, sever-

al of his friends including myself, invited him
to the parlor of the hotel and presented him
with a diamond shirtstud. We had a royal time
of it that night, and I took occasion to ask him
quietly how it was that he got over the widow's
objection to his marrying her daughter—on account of his poverty. He told me that the
story was too long to relate then, but after he
got settled in the West he would send me a long
letter giving me a truthful account of how he
'struck it.' Mulligan was as good as his word,
and sent me this package."

Dead Man's Notes.—That gentleman then seized the fire-tongs and
with averted face grasped the package and holding it at
arm's length laid it in the Lawyer's lap.

The Engineer took a wad of paper from his
pistol pocket which action seemed to relieve the
company greatly as the bulge had looked suspicious, and tossed it to the Host, who shuddered
and dodged as the bundle dropped to the floor.
That gentleman then seized the fire-tongs and
with averted face grasped the package and holding it at arm's length laid it in the Lawyer's lap.
He in turn trembled and became pale, but as no

one offered to relieve him he opened the package. A rising voice being taken as to whether or not he should read it, he was left sitting, the other chairmen declaring that the thing was carried with "unanimous animosity."

The Lawyer cleared his throat and began faltering through the awful recital. Happily his voice grew stronger as he proceeded in reading the narrative of

THE DEAD MAN'S NOTES.

I am a mail clerk. Any person who would take even a casual glance at me would surmise at once that if a clerk at all I was a male clerk, but no one would take me to be a clerk by the smallness and softness of my hands, because they are neither small nor soft. I am a believer in the sentiment of the old song, "A fig for your lord with his soft silken hand," for I am both hard-fisted and hard-headed and can give and take as much in the way of hard knocks as most men.

To begin with, I was born quite young, like most fellows, and owing to the early death of my parents was left to shift for myself. As long as I can remember, my life has been one of bustle and hustle up to a week before I married my present wife, Mrs. Mulligan, if you please. Then the event occurred which forms the subject of this little story, and which was the foundation of my present serenity and the first real streak of what little financial success I ever reached.

As I have stated I have been hustling since I was born, and worked at whatsoever my hands found to do. From a bootblack to a newsboy, then an errand boy in an office, a butcher's assistant ; I did a horse's work in a grocery, was a stripper in a tobacco house, a farmer's help, a factory hand, a boat builder, a porter, a printer, a clerk, in fact I worked at about everything in turn and was nothing long except poor. The reason I followed these various employments was not because I was not apt to learn the proper use of hands and head, but because I could not afford to be idle and when one thing failed I took up another. It was work or starve with me and of the two evils I chose the least. I think the bulk of my time was spent in a country printing office, where I started as a " devil " and raised—Cain. Here I arose to the dignity of a " sub," on one or two memorable occasions, when the editor's wife was ill and the rest of the office had gone to the circus on free passes. During my stay in the printing office I took up the study of telegraphy by the Morse system, and tackled stenography having found a discarded book on that subject in the lodging house where I stopped. While employed in the printing-office as a " galley " slave, I pursued this study assiduously, but never reached any very alarming speed, although I could read notes well, in fact, in a manner surprising to myself.

Indeed, the more obtuse the notes seemed, the better I liked them, and unless they were absolutely shocking I could generally make a fair transcript. As I say I never could write with anything like half speed. I not only could read bad notes but could decipher probably the worst writing that was ever handed in to a newspaper office, and, I think, the most execrable scrawls ever made are those that come into the office of a country newspaper. When anything unusually atrocious reached us, on which the compositors failed, my services were called into requisition and I do not now remember an instance where I failed to make out, if not exactly what the writer meant, something so near it, that I never heard any complaint.

Puzzles in writing, rebuses, riddles and cryptographs were my delight, and the more abstruse, the more pleasant to me when I got at the hidden meaning. This faculty or facility, if it may be called so, made me somewhat famous on a small scale, and through the influence of a friend, I was billetted on the post-office of —— as an assorting clerk where my known skill in deciphering poor writing was put to the severest tests. My singular facility in this direction was soon observed by my superiors, and I was in demand. Becoming proud of this appreciation of my ability, I began to dip into the subject deeply.

I studied cipher codes, I endeavored to unravel cryptographs or cryptograms and various methods of secret communication I took a shy at, and was much interested in the subject.

During this course of study I formed the theory which I believe to be the true one, that there is no system of secret communication which cannot be deciphered if one has the patience to keep at it.

In other words, I am a strict believer in the authority that holds it to be doubtful whether human ingenuity can construct an enigma of a kind which human ingenuity cannot by proper application resolve.

There is a key to every lock and it can be found by a diligent and persevering search. I felt confident of this and encouraged by it; and, many a night while other young men of my acquaintance were off at a ball or a theatre seeking legitimate recreation after the labors of the day, I spent poring over some wretched code or mystery in writing, which even when unraveled was not worth the candle.

CHAPTER VII.

THE DEAD MAN'S NOTES—*Continued.*

DURING my stay at the post-office at ——— a middle-aged gentleman frequently called for mail addressed to the office to Charles H. Rumsby as he described himself to be, and on several occasions I was at the delivery window as relief clerk when the man whose duty it was to attend there was absent or otherwise engaged.

After this party had called for mail two or three times, I began to know him, and could always inform him as he came up to the door-way, even before he approached my window, whether there was anything for him. Once or twice I saw postal cards addressed to him written in a system of stenography that I knew something of. I was pleased to know that he was acquainted with the art and pleasantly bid him the time of day when he called. The fact that he received such cards convinced me that he was one of the craft, and we struck up quite an acquaintance.

If the truth must be told I sometimes looked at the message on such postal cards ; I do not say that this was fair or even decent. But while it would be despicable or perhaps dishonorable in another person it was, I think, justifiable in my case (I was authorized sometimes to open even enclosed letters and read them), and having this craze I tell you about for detecting the medium used in secret communications I thought perhaps—well, the question of ethics I will not go into now. I do say this, however, I never read a card sent to another person which had been written in good, plain handwriting. But the moment I saw anything like an attempt of secrecy, I confess, I did try to get at the bottom of it, not to serve any object of my own, but just to know—on the principle, I suppose, that forbidden fruit is always the sweetest.

I think it was on the last occasion when Mr. Rumsby called for mail, that I was at the delivery window. He was accompanied on that call by a tall young man. I had a postal card for him covered with stenographic characters, and handed it out. He took it, read it, and gave it to the other party, saying, "Look here, Smith." Both laughed and walked off. I naturally concluded at once that his friend was an artist in crooks and curves also. The incident was soon out of my mind.

Some months after that I was promoted to the position of mail clerk on the G. O. P. Railroad, where we took on all the mail for the general P. O. at ———. It was my duty to sort and classify this mail matter en route. When not engaged in this work I could read the papers, smoke, chat or pass the time in whatever way suited my fancy.

Now, I am no great hand to read newspapers, strange to say, but it happened that I found a half sheet of the New York *Sun* which some passenger had thrown in a vacant seat in one of the cars, and as I was at leisure I took a glance at it. I was about to throw it aside, when one paragraph caught my eye. It was this:

"The drowned body of the man taken from the water off Sandy Beach as stated in these columns last Tuesday, was identified as that of Charles H. Rumsby, a resident of Phillipsburgh. It is not known positively whether the drowning was the result of accident or a deliberate suicide. The fact that the dead man's clothing, containing his papers and valuables was left in the bathing-house, would seem to set at rest the suicide theory. It is said that the deceased carried a large amount of insurance on his life. The Coroner was notified."

I started to think where I had heard that name, and after a minute's pause it came to me; it was the gentleman who used to call for the

Mull. puzzled.

mail at ———, the man who got the postal cards in short hand. "Poor fellow," I thought, "that ends it all."

I dismissed the subject from my mind, or thought I had done so. I started after we took on the bag at ——— to sort the mail, and found in it one postal card in short hand, but not apparently in any system with which I was ac-

quainted, and addressed to some one named
Smith. I laid it aside, intending to take another
look at it when I had more leisure, but Engineer
Whitcomb and others came in and began talking about that widow, the fine eyes she had, &c.,
and before I knew the mail bag had to be locked
so as to be "snatched" at the next station, and
it was time to put the card in. I would have
liked to read it, but could not delay its delivery,
even to satisfy my curiosity.

I merely mention the fact of receiving that
card here because it brought to my mind vividly
poor Rumsby and his calling at my window at
the office so hale and hearty a few weeks before.
Well, I got thinking over this, and do you know
I went and got the scrap of paper I had been
reading and looked at the date. It was the 15th;
that was Friday. The "Tuesday last" referred
to in the account was the 12th. I became interested, tried all I could to get the paper of the
12th, and after some difficulty succeeded. Opening it quickly my eyes soon caught the heading,
"A Sad Case of Drowning." I read it carefully,
but gleaned no additional facts from the account. It differed in no particular from what I
had read in the issue of the 15th, save in the
statement that the deceased was accompanied to
the watering place by Mr. J. L. Smith, and was
unmarried ; that he was an expert swimmer,
and it was supposed that he was carried out by
the undertow and met his death as above stated.

I was in doubt whether to try and forget the
whole thing or to go into it deeper. I was convinced now that the deceased was my chance
acquaintance of the post office window, and that

the Smith who accompanied him on the fatal day was the young fellow to whom he had shown the postal card the last time I had seen him alive. I was really grieved for the poor gentleman.

Carried out, I thought, by the undertow, to die a lonely, horrible death in the awful expanse of the angry waters. Above him the sky, and about him the cold, treacherous, unfathomed and relentless waves, in whose awful roar the shriek of the exhausted, dying man was lost.

Oh ! it was terrible !

The mere fact that he was a dextrous swimmer simply prolonged his sufferings.

I endeavored again to dismiss the subject from my mind, but as much as I tried it seemed to be utterly impossible.

The hideous picture of the strong swimmer in his agony, the gallant struggle in the seething waters, the final gasp of the exhausted man, the white face and stiffened form tossed about on the mountainous waves of the ocean, and finally the ghastly, bloated, stiffened corpse thrown up on the beach at Sandy Bar—I shuddered. The more I endeavored to get rid of it the worse it got. I even think that I would have attended the inquest, but as my duties did not permit me to do this I did the next best or worst thing, that is, invested in a daily paper and read the proceedings before the Coroner.

The account was quite short. J. L. Smith deposed that he accompanied the deceased to the beach ; that the deceased went in for a bath ; swam some distance beyond the safety lines ; then he suddenly threw up his hands with a shriek, and that was all.

By the time he (witness) had found and notified the bathing-house keeper, who in turn had
found the life saver, who in turn had found the
life boat, and had gone to where the deceased
had disappeared, there was nothing to be seen,
of course. And I said to myself, sarcastically,
Of course not! Oh, no! The deceased left no
hole in the water, not even a note on the waves,
or an anchored buoy, or anything by which he
could be traced; and the jury returned the same
old verdict of "accidental drowning." In my
opinion if they would hang a bathing house
keeper or two for malfeasance, or misfeasance,
or nonfeasance, or something, or even fine them
fifty dollars and collect the hard cash for every
time some poor creature lost his life under such
circumstances, because the appliances or remedy
for life-saving (that is, the man and the boat)
are not on hand when wanted, it would reduce
the accidental drownings at watering places by
about ninety-five per cent.

I wrote this when the thing occurred and I was
hot and full of the subject, having heard of so
many such casualties, and I hope you will pardon
me for this angry digression.

There was one little statement in the account
of the inquest that made me mad—yes, mad!
It was this : "The proceedings were watched by
Shrewd & Grippe, attorneys for various life insurance companies in whom it is said the deceased had policies on his life for a large amount."

I finished reading the account and tried again
to dismiss the whole thing from my mind; I
tossed the paper out of the car window; I wanted
to forget it. I might as well try to fly.

You know the trouble which a person sometimes has to get rid of a distasteful thought, or
of a tune which you hate yet catch yourself
whistling or humming. You stop suddenly, disgusted at yourself, and determined not to, and in
less than two minutes you are at it again. That
was my case exactly about this matter. Then I
took the other course, and devoted all my spare
time to it—went into it thoroughly, thinking
that perhaps I could wear the thing out by that
means. I eagerly scanned the papers for any
further account of the case, and after a while
found about two lines in the New York *Herald*
to the effect that "the policies had not yet been
paid on the life of the late Charles H. Rumsby
to Mr. J. L. Smith, the dead man's beneficiary,
as the companies were not wholly satisfied." I
laughed at this, wondering what would satisfy
companies in paying out money. There were
the policies, premiums all paid and regular, and
the man's dead body. Of course, I said, they
were corporations, and if they could prove that
the man had been killed several years previously
in a railroad accident, or that such a person had
never existed, or had died in infancy it might
work. But they had collected the premiums
steadily when due, you see. Ah ! that's a different thing ! They took the man's money right
along, and when he wanted his, or his folks did,
there was trouble. So, I says, no wonder people
sometimes remark that corporations have no
souls.

Well, I had begun to get tired of the whole
matter, and I thought it was getting faint in my
mind. In a week or two, I dare say, it would

have faded away altogether. Then something happened that set my brain working and my nerves tingling.

While sorting the mail a day or two afterwards I saw a thing and I could hardly tell you what it was. This is what it appeared to be: a U. S. postal card addressed to J. L. Smith, Phillipsburgh, postmarked St. Louis, with a stenographic message on the reverse side.

This card which I held in my hand was as follows :

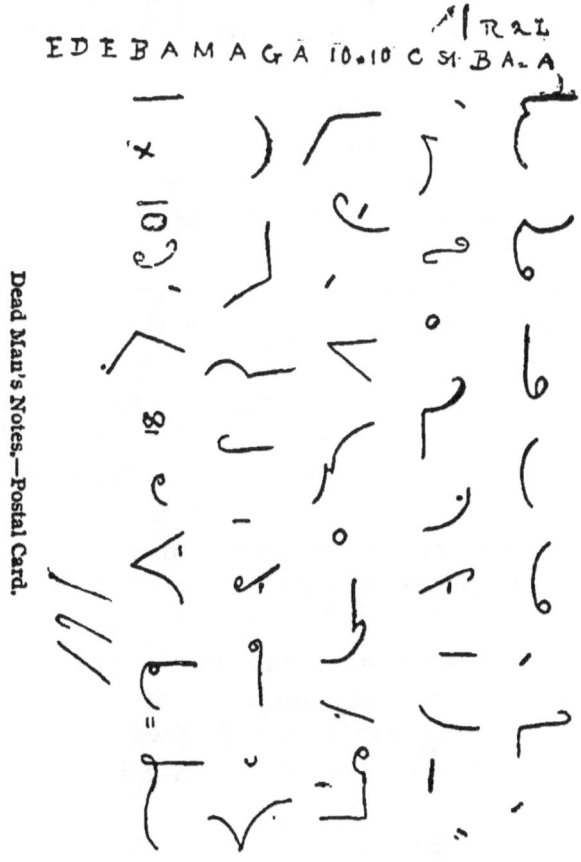

Smith, as I remembered, was the name of the witness in the Rumsby drowning case—the young man who accompanied the deceased to my post-office window and who laughed so pleasantly at poor Rumsby's short hand message.

I looked at this with all my old curiosity excited, and I must confess I did not read it readily. This only stimulated me to get at the bottom facts which I proceeded to do.

I scrutinized it steadily for several minutes. Then, fearing to be interrupted by Whitcomb or some of the others passing through the car, and desiring time to investigate, I searched my pocketbook for a small piece of tracing paper or cloth which I thought I had.

Having found it I laid it over the card and taking my pencil carefully traced the notes as they appeared through the semi-transparent cloth.

This copy I cautiously placed in my pocketbook and again took up the card to study the message. It was well I had made the copy.

Scarcely had I seated myself card in hand again when two or three parties came in to chat. Although desiring much to be left alone I could not order them out ; nor did I care to be seen reading the mail before them, and, as I could do nothing at the time I put the card in the mail bag.

During that whole day so pre-occupied was I with cogitation on the subject that I was not as quick in sorting as usual and it was all I could do to get the mail ready for "snatching" at the way station.

When my duty for the day ended I could

scarcely wait to eat before I was up in the quiet of my own little room with a lamp, a magnifying glass and such things as I might need. It was with a thrill of delight that I took out my facsimile of the card and placed it on the little table.

As a matter of extra precaution I began first and made two more copies of the tracing and had the fourth about completed when I discovered that I could read the message in a way.

This is not surprising. I had looked at it in the course of the day perhaps twenty times; had written or traced it four times, so it was no wonder that I read it : but as I say, in a way, that is to say, I failed to make good sense out of it. I carefully wrote down the transcript as I made it out on this shape :

| R , L

" EDEBAMAGA 10—10 C S1 B A—A

" Divine science gives no influence to direct to the home. Strife is overcome here below ; it shall get the deep ocean to tarry, for the Lord is giver. Each syndicate may keep death down, but pains secure would feel it.

" 10 verse, on Chap. S1 St. Paul. Addison-Testimony 161."

I read, re-read, studied, worried and pondered over that blessed thing for four mortal hours. It was in vain. I could make nothing else out of it.

Not being sure that even this was the correct or the apparently correct reading I determined to have that question settled at once.

Before going on duty next day I took one of the tracings to Mr. David McKoon, a well known stenographer, who roomed with others of the same calling in the Jones Building. Requesting a transcript of the notes I promised to call for it in a few hours which I did.

I do not know, of course, what difficulty that gentleman or his associates had with the cipher but the transcript furnished me was substantially as I had already made it with the difference of a word or two.

As easy as print—" By the Card."

The same request to others of McKoon's profession brought from some that it could not be read, it was "jargon" or "buncombe." Others read it in part, and still others made the transcript or meaning somewhat as McKoon and myself had made it.

I was by no means sure as I say that even this was correct.

Looking at the foot of the message I observed what I supposed was a reference to a certain verse and chapter of St. Paul. I then submitted it to certain newspaper reporters assuming of course that they would be thoroughly acquainted with Holy Writ. One of them was too busy to bother with it. Two or three others could not understand what I meant by the " Scriptures." One quoted a passage from Shakespeare and insisted in solemn earnest that it was such and such a chapter and verse of the Book.

Still another began as he thought to quote the Bible and got in " Now he laid him down to sleep," &c., as a certain portion of it.

I even tackled a very clever journalist from Chicago, asking him if he knew anything about St. Paul. Upon his answer that it was a regular one-horse place away behind " our town," I gave the thing up in disgust and started to do myself, what I should have done in the first place, that is : follow the advice of my poor old mother, "Search the Scriptures."

Well, I searched and searched till grey day came in through the window blinds in the morning. I found nothing in St. Paul, or any other epistle or gospel, or anything in the New or Old Testament that seemed to be at all like it.

I then turned to Addison, and went through the " Spectator," looking for " testimony," anything and everything from his poems and essays that I could lay hands on. In vain.

I then counted the words, read them in columns, or tried to, upside down, forwards and backwards, counted the letters ; took the first letter of each word in the transcript, the last, and the middle. It was all useless, and I was just where I started.

I was utterly baffled, I confess, by the abstruseness of this seemingly simple message.

I remembered reading somewhere that to master a thing of this kind the way is to read, if you can, the connected legible characters, and then the difficulty of the thing disappears ; otherwise, there is no alternative but experiment, directed by the probabilities of every device known to him who attempts the solution, till the true one is attained.

On the whole, this did not seem to be very encouraging, but my course was to keep on.

I looked long and carefully at the top of the message, at what McKoon, myself, and others had made out to be "odd," or " due, R : L." The conclusion I reached was that this meant " odd, right to left." I tried to apply it. No go. Disheartened and vanquished, I thought of giving it up, but reconsidered it. No; you were never yet beaten by any secret code, I said to myself ; you must conquer or burst, Tom, and you never burst. Tried it again—the same result. I own I was dispirited to the verge of despair. I have one recourse always to fall back on when everything else fails. I believe it has pulled me through when I had many a close call. That is, prayer.

Oh! you wretched skeptic; you needn't laugh. Try it in a pinch, and if there is no God, the prayer won't hurt you ; if there is, you may get help.

I admit that this is a poor argument, yet, it is the only one that reaches *some* people.

And, surely, the being who made us is willing to aid even such poor creatures as we are, if he is :

> " Who sees with equal eye, the God of all,
> A hero perish and a sparrow fall."

I knelt down to it—Whitcomb, you know that my faith is not exactly the same as yours ; older, perhaps—but, as I say, I knelt down, invoked help, got up and looked at that insignificant bit of tracing paper again. I intended to fix it in my mind before I went to bed, so that by chance I might dream out the meaning. I turned it, and—— Oh! by the Lord Harry, I had it.

I gave one whoop, and then I shook hands with myself, in imagination. Then I sat down and had a good comfortable smoke, wrote the true transcript out, placed it with the other papers and retired.

CHAPTER VIII.

THE DEAD MAN'S NOTES.—*Continued*.

IT was some time before I dropped off. I felt the bed shaking under me as I burst out into the most dreadful fits of laughter. I must have spent an hour or two giggling at the newspaper men, at the stenographer, at everything and everybody, including "Yours truly," and at times felt like kicking myself, because I didn't see it before. So palpable, too.

Next morning, bright and early, I got a letter of introduction to and was at the office of Shrewd & Grippe, the lawyers for the Payupsoon Life Assurance Company, and after what I thought was an interminable wait, the senior partner came in.

After the usual salutations, I asked him if the company which his firm represented had paid up the policies on the life of Peter Johnson, or any other person who had lost his life by drowning, and, I added, " or was said to have lost it."

The old lawyer looked at me cautiously and inquiringly. I am not so simple ; I said nothing further, just then.

He called in his partner and they both got at me, wanting to know what I meant.

I said this : "I desire to know, gentlemen, if anything is to be paid, and if so, how much, to the heirs of Jones, for instance, or his representatives, if he is really dead, and assuming that he had his life insured in such a company.

"If he is not dead, as claimed," I went on,

"and conclusive proof of his existence is given to the company, is the person who furnishes that information entitled to, and will he receive, any recompense for furnishing information of the existence of the insured, and if so, how much?"

The younger lawyer, Mr. Grippe, jumped up, all excitement, and shot off his jaw too soon. He blurted out: "Do you know anything about it? Where is this Charles H. Rumsby, anyhow?"

I said, "Who?" with a deprecating smile, and what I meant to be a blank look of innocent inquiry, that I think convinced the lawyers they had no fool to deal with.

The senior member, turning to the other, said something in a low tone, and then approaching me, earnestly remarked:

"Young man, you seem to be a discreet, shrewd and deserving person. It may be that you are justified in asking the question, a question which, from another person, we would consider highly impertinent; but, as it is a matter of public knowledge, I feel at liberty to say this much, in strict confidence, to you:

"The amount involved in the Rumsby case, which, I doubt not, is the case which you are talking *at*, is $75,000.

"The companies have thus far refused payment of the claim, in the honest belief that the assured is not dead. They have now no other legal or technical ground on which to resist the payment of it.

"We are interested especially in the ——— company, and it may be, that if the officers of that company can obtain satisfactory proof which will enable them to resist, honestly and honorably, mind you, the payment of the amount of the policy which the assured held in that company—$28,000—it is possible that some such arrangement as that you speak of might be made.

"In all probability," the lawyer went on, "that case will settle the others, and I have no doubt that if the proof is satisfactory and conclusive, the companies will be fair—yes, liberal with you. Please remain seated."

Well, I waited. In less than thirty minutes the President of the ——— Insurance Company came in, in a state of great excitement, puffing and blowing like a porpoise.

The matter was cautiously gone over by the lawyer. He said in substance to the president, that this young man (myself) had called, bearing a letter of introduction from a friend, and he (the young man) thought he could perhaps show where there was a fraud being perpetrated or attempted on the company. Of course, it was only right that if he did so—furnished conclusive information of that fact and saved the companies the payment of a large amount of money —he should be compensated.

The president listened and bobbed his head up and down over his gold-headed cane at every word.

He looked at me earnestly, and asked was I the person. I answered in the affirmative, and hastened to assure him that I knew what I was talking about.

The president then remarked: "Young man, a reward has already been offered in this case of $3,000 for proof such as you claim you have.

"That amount was offered by our own company, which has the most at stake.

"It is true that a drowned body was recovered which was said to answer the description of the insured person, but so far as we can learn there has been no conclusive identification.

"I trust I do not discourage you too much, young man, when I state that I believe it to be among the bare possibilities only, that you should succeed in furnishing a clue where others, including some of the most expert detectives, have failed so signally.

"But, assuming that you succeed, I think I can safely promise the amount that I have already mentioned on behalf of our company, and fully as much more on behalf of the others. Of course, sir, before we lose any time on the question of compensation, we would like to know what is the nature of the proof which you deem so conclusive and of which you are so confident."

"Draw up a paper," I answered, "and make it short and strong first, and after the paper is ready and signed, I will tell you."

The president, after a thoughtful pause, said : "This is a very unusual proceeding, sir, but if I consent to this, I cannot bind the company ; I will bind myself personally, and will sign such a paper; but it must be with the provision that if the information is of such a character as to be vague, unsatisfactory or useless, that my written promise is not binding——"

"We will take care of that," interrupted the lawyer.

Well, after some further hesitation, a paper

was drawn up by which I was to get $6,000 if the proof was such as to enable the insurance companies to successfully resist the payment of "Policies Nos. 109511 and 51736 alleged to be due the legal heirs or representatives of one Charles H. Rumsby, alleged to be dead."

I read the paper over carefully, after which the lawyer put an endorsement on it, and placed it in his safe "in escrow," he said, whatever that may mean. He then motioned us to proceed with our conversation. I looked at them.

"Now, sir," said the president, "you feel doubtless secure, but I assure you you would be equally so relying on my word. Now, as to the nature of your information. Is it such as will ——"

"It is the man himself," I cried, with a rising inflection, and I could scarcely keep down my voice in my excitement.

"How? where? when?" inquired the old lawyer, rising.

The president seemed to be struck helpless.

"I have his address," I answered. "The man, Charles H. Rumsby, is alive and well; I have seen a postal card from him since his alleged death. You have nothing to do but take an officer, go to his address, and put your hands upon him."

The lawyer whistled. The president's mouth opened wide with astonishment and his eyes danced for joy.

"Where, where, where, is this proof. How did you come by it?" he cried.

I took out my tracing paper, and represented first that it was the fac simile of a postal card addressed to one J. L. Smith. I produced the testimony adduced at the inquest to show that this Smith was the person who accompanied Rumsby to Sandy Beach on the supposed fatal Sunday. I showed them that the card was written as the post-mark indicated, eleven days after the alleged death, and posted in St. Louis as "a blind." I asserted that it was written by the assured, and that his address was 1072 Beach Street, St. Paul, Minn., where he was quietly awaiting the collection of the "soap," and if they wanted him at once they had only to say the word.

After some further talk at the request of the president, I went over the whole thing in minute detail and stated my theory to them. To judge by the way the insurance man nodded he was convinced of its truth.

CHAPTER IX.

THE DEAD MAN'S NOTES.—*Concluded.*

MY statement or theory was this : Two of the conspirators, Rumsby and Smith, went to the beach to bathe, and were seen to enter the water together, after having procured bathing suits and disrobing. Rumsby, an exceedingly expert swimmer, floated out of sight of the hundreds of bathers, who in truth paid but little attention to him. He left his clothing, valuables and trinkets in the bathing-house, and his adroit friend was on hand to give the alarm at the proper time.

Silently and surely the insured made his way by strong swimming to a distant rowboat which if seen from the shore at all appeared to be the merest speck upon the waters. Reaching the "off shore" side of the boat the swimmer was quickly helped on board. Willing hands aided him to to take off the bathing suit, which was at once placed on a "cadaver" that was ready to hand, furnished by Dr. Smith. The key of the bathing house was taken from the wrist of Rumsby and buckled on the stiff arm of the corpse. The "cadaver" was of such size and general appearance that after the buffetting of the waters, the work of the crabs and fishes it passed without question for the body of the missing man.

While the insured was clothing himself at his leisure with the apparel provided for him in the yawl it was rowed out still further. The body of the unknown dead was then cast into the deep. After making a wide detour the conspirators landed miles below the point where several days afterwards the body was picked up.

The distracted friend Smith, when the proper time came and his companion disappeared, had nothing to do under the circumstances but describe the death cry he deposed to, and the sinking of the sturdy swimmer which of course he did.

Strangely enough others present at the beach first hinted and then insisted that they observed something of the kind. As you know it is not uncommon when anything dreadfully horrifying takes place that some who know nothing of the occurrence rush to the front (perhaps to get their names in print), and vehemently assert that they were there and saw it. In time they tell it so often they really believe they are telling the truth. So it was in this case.

The bruised, swollen and fish-eaten body was thrown on the beach by the incoming tide two days subsequently as described in the newspapers.

The bathing-house keeper and his assistants identified the key that hung on the dead man's arm, and the bathing suit in which the stiff body was clothed. They insisted with some degree of positiveness that the drowned body was that of the man who so foolishly and despite all warnings ventured beyond the life lines and was lost through his own carelessness.

The great fact that Smith recognized and positively identified the body of his friend, that Rumsby was not seen again, taken in connection with the papers and valuables found in the clothing in the bath-house, the key of which was still on the body, and the other circumstances, not forgetting the hysterical and agonizing sorrow of Smith, would be quite enough to convince anyone as it did the coroner's jury, of Mr. Rumsby's death by drowning.

Of course there was no doubt of it.

There was but one question : whether it was suicidal or accidental.

The coroner's jury mercifully held to the latter theory and rendered the somewhat stereotyped but obviously just and proper verdict that appeared in the daily papers under the heading of "A sad case of accidental drowning."

The arch conspirator from his distant hiding place in the West to which he had proceeded on the afternoon of the "fatal" day, not having heard from his friend and beneficiary became a little anxious to find out just how matters stood, and hence wrote the cipher card to Smith renewing his promise to share the "soap" and all that.

It was the crudest thing in the world.

Any one with his eyes in his head, if he had a head fit to hold eyes, could see through it at a glance.

Here it is in extenso.

To the obtuse this is abstruse ; yet how obvious.

A "house afire" is not more apparent, nor the nasal appendage affixed to your countenance. You can see it at once if you know just how to look.

The clever fellow locked up the secret but

EDEBAMAGA 10.10 C S1 B A. A

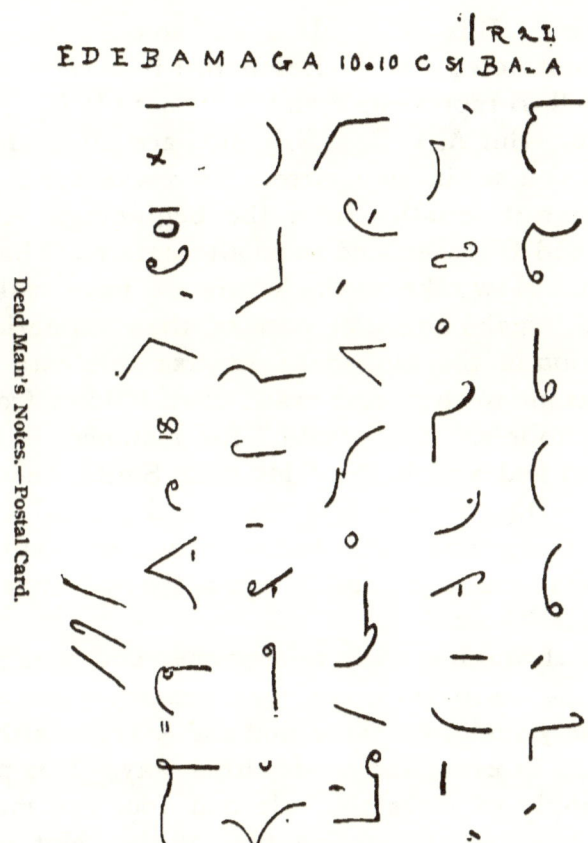

foolishly left the key in the lock.   Don't you perceive it yet?   Well, look at this:

EDEBAMAGA 10—10 C S1 B A—A

" What is that perpendicular stroke before the first R—R, 2, L ?"   It is the character for " odd."

"What is odd ?"   In this case a number that cannot be divided by 2 without a fraction or re-mainder.   But these are letters, you say.   Just so.   Consider that the letters are numbers and what have you ?

A is 1 ; B is 2 C, 3 ; D, 4, and so on.

See it now ? No ? Let us test it once more.

Well, B represents 2 and is even so is D, 4, F, 6, etc. But A, 1, C, 3, E, 5, etc., are all "odd." Now you see it, of course. To make sure, go through it seriatim from the beginning. A is odd and B is even, and so on alternately. That's plain. Now take all the letters we have called "odd," make a mental note of their numerical position in the alphabet ; reverse this card as you come to them and read what follows from right to left. E (5) "odd," for instance, is re versed and you have: " My dear Smith, secure my "—D (4) is even, and read in the usual way is: "things and direct to." Then a misleading comma, and A (1) " odd " again, " new." Invert- ed it is " home."

Go through it all in this manner and you see at a glance that it is really elementary if not ab- solutely shallow. Note that the A (1) is either " odd " or even, and reads either way. It is put in simply to prove the rule and fool the mule that attempts to resolve the tangle. Not me. The sagacious old lawyer saw through it in less than two minutes. And the initials of the sig- nature "Chay Hay Ray" "C. H. R." resemble so much " 161," yet that in itself is what the boys call "a dead give away." And Oh! the patient way in which I pored and studied over " Addison's Spectator," and looked for " testimony " to find the meaning of one word written twice, when by the application of this simple device I could see with half an eye it was " Minnesota." It makes me savage even now to think of it.

Now apply the key to the lock and try it. Insert it carefully and turn. Don't you hear the click ?

Ah ! it is open, as you see. The obscuration is dispelled. Look :

"My Dear Smith, secure my things and direct to the new address as given. Did they get the body alone all right in the way as figured ? Are documents in ? Keep shady till the soap comes. We share it.
1072 Beech St., St. Paul, Minnesota. Ch. H. R."

To make it "more definite and certain," as the lawyers said, and so intelligible that he who runs may read, let us put it in good plain print, inverting the words as they are inverted in the cipher. Put your eye on this :

Dear My Smith secure my things and direct to the new address as given here below. Did they get the way the in right all alone body ? figured 'Keep shady till the soap comes we. share it.
    or seven 2 Beech St St. Paul, Minnesota,
            Ch. H. R.

The initials of the signature "Chay Hay Ray" I took for 161—so dreadfully like it—but a great poet has truly said : "And things are not what they seem." I agree with him. "Addison" and "testimony" are simply two ways of writing "Minnesota." Turn the lower part of the card up and look.

Well, that is all.

I made out the cipher to the satisfaction of the interested companies. The conspiracy collapsed like a bursted soap bubble. Neither the "dead" man nor his beneficiary got the money on the policies. Smith was not arrested, nor was anything done to apprehend his "pal," Rumsby. They were clever fellows, both ; and, somehow or other, suspecting there was something in the wind, "lit out."

Of course, the claim on the policies was not pressed to a law suit, and they never got the money. I got mine all right, and, as you know, I married the widow's daughter, and here I am as near heaven as I can be in Chicago.

———

As the Lawyer ceased reading, a loud shriek from the Host startled the company when that gentleman fell on the floor in an epileptic fit. The Coroner unloosed his clothing and, with the assistance of the others present, succeeded after a time in bringing the unfortunate gentleman to, after which the Worshipers at the Shrine of Truth solemnly adjourned.

CHAPTER X.

THE BURGLAR'S NOTES—

THE LAWYER'S STORY.

THE meeting of the worshipers was duly called to order. After some informal chat the Lawyer began :

"I am about to relate what may with propriety call an event——"

"Fable," suggested the Host, in a loud whisper, which brought a warning "sh" from the others and a disdainful glance from the Counsellor, as, scarcely pausing, he continued, "we will say it happened about twenty years ago."

"If ever," murmured the Host, and he was about to add something, but the threatening glances of the others rendered him motionless. This event, the lawyer began in a positive tone, happened about twenty years ago.

If it had occurred in any other age or country you or those of you who have brains to remember (looking steadily at the Host), would easily recall it. But in our time and land, with the multiplicity of crimes and the vast number of newspapers and periodicals that are so active in hunting down and publishing the details of sensation after sensation, it is almost impossible to remember any one such event more than a day or two, the only one in the public mind being the last one.

The occurrence I refer to was known as the robbery of the South Hampton Trust Company. For forty-eight hours the papers teemed with accounts of it, but the blowing up of that steamboat on Lake Erie, in which so many passengers were drowned, overshadowed the occurrence I mention.

This most gigantic burglary was committed between the hours of 10 o'clock on a Sunday night and 6 A. M. on Monday. The roundsman who had just come on post discovered the janitor of the building, bound hand and foot, lying across the doorway of the bank. The man was gagged and unconscious. The blood streamed from an ugly cut in his forehead, made, as the officer conjectured, by a "jimmy."

The "burglar proof" safe was discovered wide open, the heavy iron door broken from its hinges, and the wards of the locks bent and battered out of shape.

Over $500,000 in cash, besides a large quantity of negotiable and non-negotiable securities, aggregating in total a vast amount—nearly a million dollars in cash and notes—were taken.

The Scribe here broke in : "I perceive you are going to show that a stenographer was the guilty party."

The Lawyer spoke up with some asperity : "Am I not to be allowed to proceed in an orderly manner? Why anticipate?"

The abashed Stenographer said hurriedly: "Oh, certainly—excuse me; I simply inferred that was the idea, because a stenographer would be the only one to take notes."

The Coroner was on his feet in an instant. "I protest," he said, with some heat, "against any further interruption. We listened quietly to your very transparent fanlight matter, and if this is going to continue it may become my official duty to sit on somebody."

In profound silence the narrator resumed: "Humming Bird and Howl was the law firm for whom I was managing clerk at the time—the well-known criminal lawyers——"

The irrepressible Host inquired: "Ah, did you become one——"

"Do not interrupt me, sir," said the Lawyer in a lofty tone. "I was about to say well-known criminal lawyers—meaning lawyers who appeared, when retained, for criminals, and also for innocent persons accused of crime."

We were retained by a client who had nearly $40,000 worth of securities among those that had been feloniously taken from the bank vaults, and armed with a letter of authority from our firm, I waited on the Trust Company's officials within an hour or two after the discovery of the crime.

When I arrived there I found everyone in a state of excitement. On the street a lot of newspaper men were cooling their heels, waiting for even the smallest crumb of news for the insatiate appetite of the reading public. They were not permitted to enter the bank where there was a meeting or rather a consultation taking

place among the creditors, directors and officials,
and when I showed them for whom I was acting
I was allowed to enter the directors' room.   I
saw there the most woe-begone looking set my
eyes ever beheld.   It seemed to be assumed that
if something were not done immediately to recover the proceeds of the robbery the company
would have to close its doors at once, and it was
a question whether the bondsmen of the officials
could not be called upon to make good the de-
ficiency to the creditors to the extent at least of
these securities for whose safe keeping they were
personally responsible.   When I entered the
room a well known detective from the central
office was giving his theory of how the crime
was committed, and was listened to with profound attention.   According to his statement
there was a gleam of hope—one chance, a small
one to be sure, but a chance ; it was embraced
in this : The manner in which the burglars had
effected an entrance was well known, in fact, one
could not help knowing it, for a hole almost
large enough to drive a horse and cart through,
appeared in the wall at the southwest side of the
" strong room."   This opening led into the adjoining premises which had been for many
months and up to the night preceding the robbery, ostensibly an innocent-looking segar store.
The occupants of this store, who were supposed
to be honest but were now non-est, were a German lady, her husband and her brother. They were
gone, bag and baggage, leaving this large jagged
hole in the wall and quite a large hole in the
" resources " of the South Hampton.   It was the
detective's belief that they were members of a

gang who for some time having covetous eyes
on the well filled bank vaults had taken this
simple method of reaching the "swag." The
officer stated that although apparently conducting a quiet and respectable business they had
been in reality engaged for several months cutting through the solid three-foot wall between
the vault room and the premises which they had
hired as a vantage ground from which to work
in order to safely complete the "job." Carefully
and cautiously they had carried off the debris
until a thin partition remained between their
premises and the "strong room." He explained
all this very clearly and we saw how it was done.
The work was doubtless performed in the silent
watches of the night ; little particles of the wall
were quietly picked out piece by piece, the bricks
taken out whole, if possible or lifted out in bits.
Just below the opening there were several pieces
of old carpet and a quantity of cotton waste the
utility of which was to deaden the sound of the
falling debris. So that when particles of bricks
or mortar accidentally fell out of the wall, while
being pried out or worked at with the crow-bar
or cold chisel, if not caught by willing hands before they reached the floor they simply dropped
on this thick covering as softly and noiselessly
as bits of paper or flakes of snow. You know
what some poet says of the ballot :

> " It falls as lightly as the snow,
>   Upon the hardened winter sod ;
> And executes the freeman's wish,
>   As lightning does the will of God."

Of course this doesn't seem to apply, for the
fellows were not working out anything so sublime

as the designs of providence, but in the language of the street they "got there" as the dismantled safe, the frightened creditors, the woe-begone directors and the missing "boodle" amply testified. On the Sunday night of the robbery, the slight four inches of brick wall remaining, after the long, patient and steady work of digging, went down at once before the crow-bars of the sturdy fellows and the rest was easy. It was conjectured that the janitor, hearing the noise, was about to go into the vault room through the door way, and as he entered, one of the gang on watch, dropped a heavy bar on the unfortunate man's head, and he never knew what struck him.

Efforts had been made to revive him, with the hope that he would be able to give a description of the parties or throw some light on the matter. The man died within a day or two even while the doctors were working over him and the secret, if he possessed any, was undivulged. It seemed plain that the poor fellow's death was due to his fidelity.

The man's name was Michael O'Hara; he had been assisted in his duties by his brother James, who lived with him in a suite of rooms in the upper part of the building. Unfortunately, or perhaps fortunately for himself, James was absent on the night of the robbery and did not return till gray day in the morning. He reached the scene as the officer on post was lifting his unfortunate brother from the pool of blood which had oozed from his dreadful wound. Thus there was no one who had positive knowledge about the matter. The two employees to whom we might have looked for information, were one in a state of coma, the other in a state of total ignorance and could of course advance no facts in regard to it, so we had only the detective's theory to go upon.

At the invitation of the officer I, with others, went to the rear end of the cigar store, on a visit of inspection.

We saw the irregular hole in the wall, about three feet high by two in width, at which the burglars had evidently been working a long time. The detective showed us a nail in the wall above the opening and a torn map of the United States among the *debris*. His theory was that each night they gathered up the particles of sand, mortar or brick taken from the wall, packed it securely in cigar boxes and shipped it off as merchandise—*i. e.*, cigars.

During the day the map carefully hung over the battered wall, effectually covered the gang's work from the glance of any casual visitor, who might by chance enter the rear room of the cigar store. Of course no one would ever think of lifting up the map to see if the wall behind it was broken. The opening, in all probability, could have been made by a couple of masons in a day or two, but these shrewd fellows had worked slowly, cautiously and noiselessly, but surely, on it for seven months before they were quite satisfied. They had, without doubt, hired the premises for their felonious purpose, and, while ostensibly pursuing a legitimate business, had successfully carried out what the officer termed the " swiping of the swag."

This was so apparent as to require only the

bare statement, and the police easily obtained a description of the parties and undertook to follow them up. They, of course, had at least eight or ten hours start, and, having previously arranged their plans, knew just how to baffle pursuit. It was a "stern chase," and proverbially a "long" one. Outside of the hope of a speedy apprehension of the guilty parties, the detective's statement gave little encouragement to the directors. The valuables were gone, and how they were taken was not so important as how they could be recovered, if at all.

The investigation was a sort of Coroner's inquest—of little use to the principal party—but as a knowledge of how the job was done might throw some light on how it could be undone, the subject—the inquest—was continued. A messenger was dispatched to Shadhouse & Co.'s, the safe manufacturers, with a request that a mechanical expert be sent down to examine and report. The man sent by that firm quietly entered the room while the inspector was still detailing his theory. The officer pointed out the holes drilled in the door of the safe near the lock, in which the giant powder or dynamite was inserted, and argued that the charge was of such strength that it blew the door completely off the hinges. I agreed with him, and intimated that perhaps it was the noise of the concussion which brought the janitor to the scence of operations. The officer did not accept this theory with alacrity, but hinted that it was singular that the steady digging at the wall had been going on for many months without attracting the attention of either the janitor or his assistant.

I took a good look at the mechanic as he entered. Jackson was his name, and from the start, after closely observing his demeanor, I was favorably impressed.

He came forward when called upon by the treasurer, and, throwing his coat in a corner,

JACKSON—Making a safe conclusion.

pushed his hat down tight on the back of his head, rolled up his sleeves over a pair of brawny arms, and took a good stare at the safe. He looked at it front face and side face, took a three-quarter view, and then, lying on his back, put his head inside and looked up at what I may call the ceiling or roof of it. Then, with the aid of an assistant, he raised the iron door from the floor and put it through what I thought to be a thorough examination. Of course I did not know what it all meant, but had full confidence in the fellow. I saw he was a mechanic—an artist in his line—and while burglars, especially safe breakers, are as smart as they make them, I really believed that if there was any clew to be discovered, or any weak spot in the "job" this clear-eyed mechanic would see it. Aided by his assistant he then placed the door, as well as its battered condition would allow, in its proper position on the safe and stood silent and thoughtfully staring at the bent wards of the locks. He rubbed his fingers slowly along the nosing of the iron frame in which the wards worked, scrutinized it and tested the combination, of which this is a crude representation :

He turned the knob that was fast to and part of the inner rim and moved the hands in various directions. He then put his mouth to one of the small holes drilled in the door near the lock and, keeping the other holes closed with his finger tips, appeared by the motion of his lips and the hollows in his cheeks to be drawing air through it.

Then the assistant, under his directions, turned the door over face down on the floor, and, having placed two round balls under it, moved it about for several minutes, for the life of me I could not guess for what.

Lifting it again the mechanic bent down and scrutinized the floor with great intentness. We watched him breathlessly—I know I did—firmly convinced that he saw something with his keen, mechanical eye that was beyond our ken.

We were nearly all professional men, and thought we knew or should know much more than "a mere mechanic," but were like infants at the feet of a master—blind, groping and fumbling in the darkness, where this man saw clearly.

I was then a young fellow ; had lost nothing ; was neither disheartened nor bewildered like the others, and could look calmly and serenely on the whole proceedings ; and I was much interested in all this.

After going through this pantomime for some time he uttered one word—not even a word—it was "Huh !   then stood silent and expectant.

"Have you made any discovery ?" said one of the directors.

"Gentlemen," said Jackson, as he took out his pipe, filled it, and, after igniting a match on his thigh, lighted it, and abstractedly, as I supposed, dropped the lighted match in one of the drilled holes of the safe, "gentlemen," he said, slowly, " I cannot give you (puff) anything definite (puff) now (puff) ; I want to make a further test or two ; if I can have the use of this room half an hour I will write à report and have it ready for you some time to-day or to-morrow morning."

"Can you give us anything definite and positive ?" said a director.

"Oh," answered Jackson, with a smile, "what I give you you can bet on. Scientific theories may or may not be founded on positive facts, but mechanics must be, and are a good deal like figures, when you have them they prove themselves, and you have got something perfectly solid to rest on. I will make the written report."

We then adjourned to an adjoining room and held a secret session, not even the police officers being present.

CHAPTER XI.

THE LAWYER'S STORY.—*Continued.*

AS a lawyer representing a large creditor and depositor in the bank, who was vitally interested in the recovery of his securities, I was treated with entire confidence by the directors and my advice freely sought at this strictly private confab.

The conclusion of the directors and the sense of the meeting was this : Make every effort to recover what could be recovered—all if possible ; if not all, or if not the cash, at least the securities, or some of them.

The Trust Company people did not like to attempt this themselves—in fact did not desire to be known in the transaction—but they gave me *carte blanche* and full authority to act in the matter, with the understanding that I was to take no important step without consultation with them.

The ostensible reason for having me to act was that one of our firm was ill ; the other had, consequently, many important matters to attend to, and as the directors were somewhat dazed and unable to act cooly, some active person was needed in the emergency.

The real reason was that neither the members of our firm nor the officials cared to put themselves in the positions of "compounding a felony."

It was supposed that the negotiations to be successful would result in just this, and nothing more.

I am free to say this hypothesis was quite correct. I was to act with a detective—Reynolds, by name—and under the direction of our firm, as representing the creditor before mentioned, who was our client.

A "community of interests" is, perhaps, as strong as the "cohesive power of public plunder," and in this case it was one against the other.

Detective Reynolds.

The main point, as I say, was to avoid even the appearance of compounding a felony, an offence often committed and rarely punished, because the proof of its commission must come, in a great measure, from the party who commits it, and, therefore, it doesn't come.

That afternoon I called on the president,
Mr. Ames, and, while waiting for him, was introduced to Detective Reynolds.

We began to compare notes, and mutually
agreed on a scheme which he put in practice, of
going to the U. S. Internal Revenue Department,
to see in what district the segar dealer, Reinhardt was booked, having already got a description of the parties from the bank clerks, police
officers, and neighbors.

The Revenue books simply said, "Charles
Reinhardt; district 411; manufacturer and dealer;
factory 999."

It appeared that he had been a large pur-
chaser of revenue stamps many of which in all
probability had been used on boxes, containing
only particles of bricks and lime.

This goes to show that "the gang" did not
consider the question of expense while pursuing
their object in order to ward off suspicion.

The detective then started to go the rounds
of the segar and tobacco dealers to discover what
could be learned concerning persons answering
to the description of either of the suspected
parties. He discovered nothing that would aid
us at all.

Subsequently the president came in, and on
my asking him for the safe-expert's report, he
brought me into his private office, and with an
air of great secrecy handed out the document.

There was not much taste displayed in its
"get up." No flaming seals, or red marginal
lines or tasty blue-ribbon knots about it. No
formalities.

Not even, "know all men to whom these presents doth come." No.

None of that. It went right into the subject in this way :

"Gents : That safe of yours was neither broken open nor blown open.

"It was opened by some one who knew the combination and done in the regular way.

"It was not a combination that could be worked on chance ; there are four movements in it, each one releasing a corner of the two wards ; a man would have twenty-eight hundred and some odd movements to make before he could strike it right. So whoever opened it knew how to go about it.

" The smashing of the door was done after the stuff was taken to relieve from suspicion whoever gave the combination or opened the safe.

" The two wards on the door-lock are out of place ; the upper one forced *up*, the lower one *down*, not driven *in* or *out*. The dents at the nosing do not come where the wards strike it. They don't chime. They were shoved out of place by the blows of a sledge hammer or pried apart by a jack-screw ; most likely the latter as silent and sure.

"The holes drilled in the locks never had any powder in and were not intended for any. They don't go through the second iron plate.

"They are not deep enough and there are too many of them.

"The japan has no appearance of powder unconsumed or used ; there was none applied.

"There was no glass broken in the room, and no window left open as is generally the case when a job of that kind is finished up in a hurry.

"The holes were drilled while the door was

lying flat on the floor and *off* the hinges because the marks of the legs or clamps of the
heavy toggle lever drill show at the hinges and
they could not be inserted between the door and
frame at the hinged side if the door was *on.*

"There ain't space enough. The door was
pried off by being wedge-jammed against the
frame which broke the hinges. To conclude, I
say that safe wasn't broken open ; it was opened
in the usual way and the breaking done afterwards as a 'blind.' That is all.

"Very truly yours,
"JOHN C. JACKSON, Locksmith."

I read this over carefully, re-read, studied it
through and when I got a good mental grip of
it handed it back.

The president looked at me inquiringly, "What
do you think of that," he whispered, " can it be
by any possibility true ? "

I did not ·answer unhesitatingly or positively.
I saw that his anxiety was much greater than he
cared to admit.

He had stated to us at the meeting on the
previous day that the combination of the safe
was known only to himself and the treasurer.

As one not unfamiliar with the subtleties of the
law I supposed that ordinarily bank officials are
no more liable for the act of burglars than for
the act of God. Ill advised and excited creditors
might think differently and be disagreeable.

There were hints of carelessness in the air ;
the good name of the institution as well as the
honor and integrity of its officers was at stake.
Doubtless there were private or personal papers
or securities among those " looted " for the safe-

keeping of which both the president and treasurer were under heavy bonds. I thought of all this and concluded that suspicion could have no resting place against either of these men. In all probability they had protected their bondsmen against possible loss and in any event they would themselves be the sufferers. The theory of guilt was untenable. The slight suspicion that arose in my mind was dissipated at once. Sane men do not rob themselves.

I finally replied to his question : "Perhaps the mechanic was mistaken; his theory was so totally at variance with tnat advanced by the police that most likely Jackson was wrong."

A rap at the door interrupted us and in answer to " Come in " police officer Powers entered and laid on the desk a murderous-looking "jimmy" and a scrap of paper with some plaster still adhering to it.

The jimmy he had found in the rear of the cigar store, he said, and the paper had been firmly glued to the wall, near the opening.

In trying to peel it off with his fingers it had become slightly torn at the lower corner, so he took his pocket-knife to remove it and dug it out with patches of mortar still sticking to it.

The paper and plaster were in this shape :

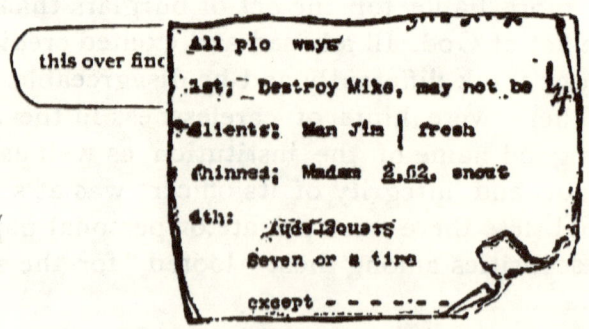

CHAPTER XII.

THE LAWYER'S STORY.—*Continued.*

OUT of curiosity I accompanied the officer to where he said he cut the paper from the wall.

I wanted to see what were the words preceding that written on the plaster, just near the edge of the paper at the left, "this over fine." I found that the wall had been so mutilated with the knife that the white mortar had entirely disappeared for some distance beyond the space where the man had taken off the lime.

I inquired if he knew or had observed whether anything else was written on the wall.

Yes, there was two or three words; he thought one was "steady," or something like it; it had an "s" in it, he believed, and he had inserted his knife far enough out to save the piece of wall the words were on, but while trying to dig it loose it broke and fell out; in his hurry to catch it before it reached the floor he grasped it too roughly in his fingers and it crumbled into sand.

After carefully taking the thickest of the plaster from the back of the paper and writing the words that appeared on the lime in his note-book, he placed the paper in his pocket-book and said he would return it to me.

He then indicated where he had found the

"jimmy," after which he went back to the president's office.

"I have a theory about this paper," the officer began, as he held it in his hand.

"Well, sir," said the president, with a faint smile, "this case bids fair to be more or less complicated by theories ; another theory cannot do it any harm. Speak up, sir."

The officer spoke hesitatingly, "I will give you the grounds of my suspicion ; if it is well founded and there is any—a—reward—assuming that my information is availed of—have I your—a—personal word that if I cannot officially make a claim you will at least—reim—er—re—member me ?"

The president nodded gravely, and the other went on ; "This paper was glued on the wall near the opening on the other side. It is, I think, some sort of secret communication, yet some of it seems plain enough. There are names here and one is "Jim" the other is "Mike."

Officer Powers paused and looked steadily at Mr. Ames.

The president remarked, "What of that ?"

"Well," said the other, "Mike was the name of the janitor, don't you see ?"

"What then ?"

"Why, he was *your* janitor."

"Tut, tut," said the president sharply, "I cannot pretend to misunderstand you, but you surely are not silly enough to claim that you have a well founded suspicion against the man who received his death wound while trying to protect the property of this institution ? That man, as I am informed, will in all probability never recover, and is even now, poor fellow, in his dying agony."

"But—" began the detective.

"Not a word, sir," said the president sternly, "the man you would point the finger of suspicion at risked his life while at his post of duty, and a suspicion that points in that direction is preposterous and baseless; nay more, it is despicable and mean to the lowest degree."

The president spoke hotly, and while honoring him for it, I wanted to hear what the other had to say.

I encouraged the officer with a wink and he went on:

"If you will listen to me——"

"Even supposing," the president interrupted, "that there were something in your suspicion, if you mean to claim that he would be accessory to such a crime, there is honor among thieves and burglars do not assault each other."

"But," said the officer, "suppose it was the intention to simply stun the janitor—injure him slightly, then bind and gag him in order to avert suspicion—we have all heard of such things—perhaps it was done at his own suggestion—and that owing to the darkness, the excitement, close proximity of the person, or from some other cause, the blow was unintentionally severe, what do you say then?"

The president got on his feet, pale with anger, "I say, sir," he answered, "that your theory is ridiculous, beastly and damnable."

The police officer stood up in turn in a state of considerable excitement. "Hear me out," he cried. "There was a relative of his here, a

sort of assistant janitor named Jim, wasn't
there ? "

" There is," said the president, impatiently.
" There was ; what of that ? "

" Can you tell me," said the detective, earnestly, " how it comes that those two names are
on that paper pasted on the wall, to be seen by
no one but those who planned the robbery ?

" Why is it that the first intelligible words
here are : ' Destroy Mike.' He is the one that,
according to your statement, the attempt was
made to injure, *i. e.*, ' destroy.' Do men of that
kind write their intentions on paper and leave
the writing where it can be found, or would
they be more likely to do the very opposite ?

" They might as well have written here : ' We
will break open such and such a safe and do so
and so with the money.' Besides, the reference
to the ' man Jim,' these parties being ' clients,'
and ' fresh,' is to my mind very suggestive."

" Tut, man," answered the president contemptuously, " Jim is a very common name, and so is
Mike. There are probably thousands of men in
this great city bearing those names—aye, tens of
thousands."

" I grant you," replied the detective earnestly,
emphasizing his words with his index finger, " I
grant you that Mike is a common name and that
Jim is a common name ; still I say that the con-
junction of the names of Mike and Jim, the janitor and assistant janitor of this bank, on a piece
of paper in the hands of the gang who burglarized it is not at all common but quite unusual.
Now, what do you think ? "

The president's face was a study.

I began to see, and perhaps he did, the subtle force of the detective's argument.

"I know them both," said the president, after a pause, "I know them long and favorably as honest, faithful, hard-working men. I believe they would lay down their lives to protect this Company, and I trust that I will be the last man in the world to entertain such a dirty, despicable and damnable suspicion against these men, one of whom has shed his life-blood to defend his trust.

"But, sir, this young gentleman (pointing to myself) has been given charge of the entire matter by the directors and officials, and if he thinks it proper that you should do anything, however uncalled for, in the line of your duty, it is not for me to gainsay it. Personally, I shall not touch the matter at all," and with a gruff "good-day" the president stalked out.

I thought over it and finally concluded it would be wise to follow out the suggestions of the police officer. I applied for a warrant on papers verified by the treasurer, and before many hours passed James O'Hara was under arrest, charged, on information and belief, with being involved as accessory in the gigantic robbery of the Southampton Trust Company. I drew up, as I say, the legal papers. Like other men, I have done mean things in my life, but in all probability that was the meanest thing I ever did. When I think of it now I feel my cheeks reddening, and even now my eyes fill when I remember that I was the one who took the active steps to have a faithful man publicly charged with burglary and dragged by the officers of the law from the bosom of his little family and from the still open coffin of a dead brother who had given up his life to protect the property of his employers.

If I had any doubt of the meanness of the act at the time, I was thoroughly convinced of it when I called on James at the city prison the next day after his arrest. His wife was there with two of his little children, and if there had been an opening in the floor of that cheerless cell large enough for a rat, I think I would have tried to crawl into that hole and pull it in after me. He had been taken, as I say, from the bier of his dead brother. His wife and the widow of the dead man looked to him in their great trial as the father and common protector, and while he was locked up in jail, charged with being the aider and abettor of thieves, his friends fell off, and the poor fellow seemed to be deserted by all. Like a stranger in a strange land, he was friendless and alone.

Owing to the arrest of James there had been a complete revulsion of public feeling, even as to the dead man, a thing which often occurs and is always unaccountable. The day before, the conduct of the deceased janitor had been held up to the admiration of all as that of a faithful servant—he was spoken of in the newspapers as a martyr to duty ; now his conduct appeared in quite another light ; his untimely taking off was deplored by few or none.

The impression had gone abroad, through some channel, that he, and perhaps the surviving brother, had been concerned in the felony, and that his violent death was simply an unfortunate mistake—a miscalculation on the part of the criminals, and " served him right " was the general verdict.

Outside the widow and immediate relatives there were few mourners, and no strangers' tears were shed on the dead man's grave.

CHAPTER XIII.

THE LAWYER'S STORY.—*Continued.*

WHILE talking to James he casually remarked that the president's private stenographer knew the combination of the safe.   I
pressed him to be more explicit on this point,
and he said that he was tolerably sure that on
at least one occasion, he had seen Mr. Slocum
open it after the other clerks had left the bank.
But he (James) was not surprised, as the secretary had the privilege of the office next to the
president himself, and his authority was unques-
tioned.

James did recall that one evening, several
months previously, after banking hours, when
he was cleaning the president's room, Mr. Slocum came in in great haste saying he had lost
or destroyed a theatre ticket. It was some place
in the office and he seemed much relieved that
the contents of the waste-paper basket had not
been removed. Carefully looking through this
receptacle, the secretary gathered up several
scraps of white paper, which he said resembled
the ticket, and departed with a pleasant " good-
night."

James thought the pieces did not look much
like a theatre ticket to the best of his opinion,
but as it was not his business to interfere, he
said nothing, and would never have mentioned
the matter if I had not drawn it from him.

The following day I saw the President, Mr. Ames, and suggested to him that perchance his private secretary and stenographer knew the combination of the plundered safe. He doubted it. He was pretty positive he had not given it to any one, not even to the treasurer, but he (the treasurer) had it as it was necessary he should, having received it from the manufacturers. Yet if the janitor asserted that Stenographer Slocum had it, it was barely possible that he had given it to him. Of course, James in the vault-room, cleaning about, ought to know; but, on the whole, he thought James was mistaken. He had often opened the safe himself in the morning, and left it unlocked to enable the secretary to get papers from it, and likely enough the janitor might have seen Mr. Slocum on one of these occasions.

"Oh, by the way," he said, "the secretary has been quite ill for some days and in the excitement of this catastrophe I fear I have neglected him. I must go or ask someone to call upon him."

I cut him short by referring again to the combination of the safe. "It was sent to me," he said, "by the manufacturers in a note marked 'private and confidential' with a request that I should make a mental note of the combination and then destroy the written directions. I have no copy of it, but if you would like to see it, I will write it for you so that you can have it tomorrow, I am in haste to-day. The treasurer has a copy of it and you can see him or call in the morning and get it; it is certainly of no use to us now." Mr. Ames left me, and as I had

promised the detective the combination, though
for what purpose he wished it, I did not know.
I went to the treasurer's room and made the request.

"Oh, certainly," he said, "you can have it, it
is of no earthly consequence now, yet it is still
under lock and key."

I accompanied him to a closet, the door of
which he unlocked, and, lifting his coat from a
nail, he showed me a paper securely pasted on
the wall.

"I kept it here," he said, "fearing that I
might forget it or be taken sick during the president's absence, and it would be much easier
for me to give some authorized person the key
of the closet with directions where to look
than to write out or explain the whole combination."

I saw on the wall beneath where his coat hung
a scrap of paper which I began to copy.

"Oh," said he, "take the whole thing right
with you ; the next safe will have a different and
certainly a better combination—take it right
along with you. It is no secret now if it ever
was."

He then left and I undertook to remove the
paper by inserting my pocket-knife beneath the
edge, and finding it was likely to tear I cut
deeply into the plaster, and removed what I believed was the only written combination of the
burglarized safe in existence, outside of the office of the manufacturer. I broke away with
my fingers most of the heavy plaster attached
to it, and carefully placed the scrap in my
pocketbook, along with the paper handed me

by the police officer on the authority of which we had procured the warrant for the arrest and incarceration of the assistant janitor. This is what the treasurer told me to take from the wall.

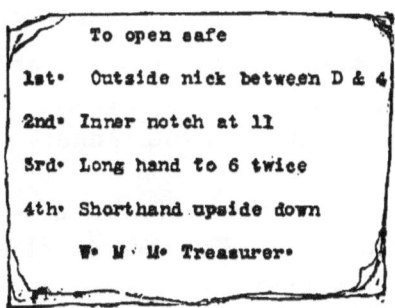

To open safe

1st· Outside nick between D & 4

2nd· Inner notch at 11

3rd· Long hand to 6 twice

4th· Shorthand upside down

W· M · M· Treasurer·

It is, as you observe, signed with his initials, and was kept securely locked in the closet beneath his office coat on the rack.

CHAPTER XIV.

THE LAWYER'S STORY.—*Continuea.*

I SAW Reynolds that afternoon and learned from him that we were at fault. There was not the slightest trace of the tenants of the adjoining store.

It was as though the ground had opened and swallowed them up. They were a clever set.

All points were watched and nothing discovered.

As a last resort, I, on my own account, inserted a "personal" in the *Herald*, promising immunity if the non-negotiable securities taken from the South Hampton Bank were returned to "X. Y. Z."

Nothing came of it.

The detective smiled sarcastically when I told him.

"You promise them immunity," he said, "a safe promise. It must make those fellows laugh. Offer them immunity, that is freedom; why they've got that now. It is ridiculous. If you had them, or one of them, safely under lock and key, you would be in a position to offer them something for something. Now you offer them nothing for something. What do you take them for? Bah!"

I was still confident, but he was right.

Nothing came of it.

I waited one more day and saw that we were just where we started.

CHAPTER XV.

THE LAWYER'S STORY.—*Continued.*

WITHIN a day or two the directors were called together and negotiations were in progress to reopen the bank for business.

I called on the president in relation to some minor formalities about it, and stated that there had been a total failure to find a clue to the guilty parties, so far, though, we were hopeful. I remarked, casually :

" I see you are getting in a new safe ; I hope it will have a combination that will not be in the hands of outsiders."

" Do you know," he said, smilingly, " that since you spoke to me about it, I have tried to remember the combination of the old safe, and I cannot seem to recall it perfectly ? "

" Why," I answered, " I have it right here in writing."

" Let me see it, for curiosity."

I opened my pocketbook and handed out the original paper, of which the detective had made a copy.

Mr. Ames looked at it and laughed. " Why this isn't it ; the treasurer didn't give you that, though it is written on our paper. I don't know what it all means—Oh," he added, " I guess that is the thing the officer took from the wall the other day, isn't it ?

" I never took a good look at it before, the

fellow vexed me so, and—by the way, you must take steps at once to release James."

I interrupted him, as, with some trepidation, I took the paper and glanced at it. Sure enough, it was what the officer had given me, on the strength of which he had made the argument followed by the warrant for and the arrest of the assistant janitor.

"Mr. Ames," I said, looking him squarely in the eye, "the release of the janitor is a matter of very little consequence just now. I will attend to that if you will answer me one question. You have just said that this was the Trust Company's paper. How do you know?

"You will understand the importance of this question when I tell you that the release of a humble, and, as you claim, an innocent man, and the clearing of his character, depend upon it. Again I repeat, how do you know?"

"I know," he replied, "by the letter-head—the lower portion of the letters in 'New York.'

"Our letter-head is like this——"

He took a sheet of the bank's note-paper, with the heading, in part :

South Hampton Trust Company,

1776 Broadway,

New York.

"The words 'New York' are in script print —you see the long tail of the 'Y,' the curl ending with a dot, and the same as to a portion of the 'k.' Look! This is what philosophers call 'ocular demonstration.'"

Lifting the scrap of paper, he placed it evenly on the letter-head sheet of the Company.

The little marks which I had before failed to notice, formed the lower portion of the stems of " $\mathcal{Y}$ " and " $\mathfrak{h}$," and fitted to a nicety. Very minute portions of the " $\mathcal{Y}or\mathfrak{h}$" appeared to be completed by letters of the same word on the letter-head.

There was no room for further doubt.

I could scarcely repress an exclamation of satisfaction. He noticed it, wonderingly.

" Is this very important ? " he asked.

"It is important in this way," I replied. " I think it tends to prove that the contention of the locksmith was well founded, and that the theory of the police was entirely erroneous. I think that is a settled fact.

" But again, the janitor is not capable of writing a thing of this kind. Whatever it means, it was written by some one in this bank.

" Somebody gave the combination to these parties, and the question is ' who did it ? ' But you and the treasurer had it.

"Neither of you gave it ; yet, this means something, and it is equally true that the Janitor, were he ever so willing, could not get up a secret code of this kind.

"Of course, I see no meaning in this tangle of words ; yet, as you say it is on the Bank paper, in the hands of the enemy, and I am convinced that—By the way, have you heard from your stenographer lately ? "

"Nothing, but that he is convalescent," he replied, " but I shall call on him——"

" No, no," I answered. " Leave it to me. I

feel convinced that we are on the eve of a discovery. Do not breathe a word of this for
twenty-four hours, and if by that time we are
not a great deal wiser than we are now, I will
throw up this whole thing."

I suddenly left the president in a brown
study.

After an interminable wait at the office Reynolds called, and in a few brief and hurried
words I made him acquainted with the late discovery, and my belief that the secretary knew
more than we at first imagined.

He did not seem much surprised at my statement, and I wondered.

He proceeded to enlighten me. "I have suspected a certain party from the first. That person was not at the bank during all the excitement following the robbery—quite ill since the
night preceding it. I 'piped' him.

"What was his object in being so ill at such a
time? Is it fear that he would inadvertently
'give away' something? Why did he go back
to the bank after business hours and pick out
scraps of paper from the waste basket as a
theatre ticket?

"Are such tickets white? How many scraps
do you think you could make out of a theatre
ticket? Why tear it? and how did he know just
where to look, or that he had torn it, and put
the scraps in that basket?

"Is a ticket of that kind a private matter that
must be destroyed? How did he happen to go
to the president's room first and find it without
looking further? Was it worth while to return
to the bank for a mere ticket that cost perhaps

not over a dollar or so ? What good were the
pieces? I have mentally dovetailed many little
circumstances, and they seem to fit into each
other perfectly on only one theory—guilt.

" Can't you get a letter from the president or
a director of the company introducing or recom-
mending a good doctor to attend the sick man
on behalf of the trustees, and at once. I can
get the doctor if you can get the letter."

Reynolds winked, and I believed I saw the
scheme.

In thirty minutes I was at the president's
house on Money Hill, and, finding him at home,
suggested the propriety of sending a physician
to the secretary's house, and after a thoughtful
pause he began to prepare the letter.

I felt that the game was in our hands.

He had it partly written, and looking up
quietly, said : " Who is the doctor ; what name ?"

" Oh, anything," I said, hurriedly, forgetting
myself, and losing sight of the importance of
doing the thing right.

He stopped with a half suspicious look at me,
and remarked : " Well, there is no use in sending
some nameless quack to see a sick person, for I
can give you a note to my family physician, a
medical man of high repute."

" Doctor Jumeau," I ejaculated desperately at
a venture. " It is a foreign name, and hard to
remember." " Well," he replied, " just as you
wish."

Then he completed and folded the letter. I
seized it, rushed out, and at the foot of the stoop
ran into the arms of Reynolds.

I scarcely knew him. He wore a pair of green

glasses, was elegantly dressed, furbished up, carried a large professional cane, and appeared to be a very sedate and prosperous looking M. D. "Have you got it," he said in a whisper.

As I placed the note in his hand he called a cab, and telling me to be at the office at 9 o'clock, started for the residence of Private Secretary Slocum, on the outskirts of the city.

I waited patiently at the down town rendezvous for him, and in about two hours he joined me.

"I was just in time," he said, in answer to my look of inquiry, "I think our bird was preparing to fly."

"I flatter myself if he had any suspicions I allayed them by telling him of the president's solicitude for his physical well-being, and as the bank was to resume on Monday morning, I was commissioned to call professionally in order to ascertain whether he could stand the strain of his regular duties.

"I think he can. He was a little doubtful himself at first, but to give his doubtfulness the benefit of the doubt I took the liberty of putting a man on up there, lest something might happen.

"Meantime prepare your papers and get out your warrant without delay—have it at an early hour in the morning."

I immediately called on the treasurer, got his verification, and soon after Court opened in the morning obtained the committment, placed the papers in the hands of an officer, and before 12.30 Mr. Private Secretary and Stenographer Slocum was in quod.

The detective had a strong impression that

the prisoner would break down and confess if
left to himself, and at the suggestion of the officer an order was left at the prison that he be
strictly secluded if possible.

We subsequently learned that he was visited
by a lawyer at his own request—this was an evil
that could not be prevented ; but from that moment the prisoner seemed to recover backbone.

CHAPTER XVI.

THE LAWYER'S STORY.—*Continued.*

ON the following day accompanied by Reynolds I called at the City prison and had a conversation with the prisoner. He seemed to take the charge of being accessory in the burglary as a cool piece of impudence on our part and hinted that he would discover the active parties and make them suffer for his unjustifiable and uncalled for arrest, and would invoke the strong arm of the law. Becoming quite vehement and indignant on this point, he called it a high-handed outrage, I think, and trusted he would have a speedy trial. He finally calmed down and said while willing to assist us in any possible way in recovering the securities, he was as innocent as the child unborn and really knew nothing, and so on.

The detective after some further conversation took a hand in the talk ; " If you are inclined to own up," he said, " restore the securities, interested parties will give all hands immunity; otherwise the law will take its course."

" That is what I desire," Mr. Slocum rejoined ; " Nothing would suit me better, because there is really no proof that I have—I do not see how an innocent man can be held for such a dastardly crime when there is really no motive. Had I been one of the guilty parties I certainly should not have waited all this time in the vicinity. Why, look at my case. Enjoying the confidence of my employers, nothing to gain and everything to lose. Would anyone suppose I should be the associate of a low gang of bank wreckers with red—red hands—I may say ; and you seem to want a man to confess when he has nothing to confess. You hint that I gave away the combination."

"Did I," said the detective quickly, "there is no use in being so quick to deny a charge of which you are not accused."

The other evidently saw, to use an expressive vulgarism, that he "put his foot in it;" still he was alert enough, too.

"Well, I heard or read in some of the papers that some one had been accused of some such thing, and that, I suppose, is what you want me to admit. I assure you, gentlemen, you are totally at fault."

"Well," remarked the detective, "suppose it was found in the possession of red—Red Jerry for instance (he had already hinted to me that the Southampton job was so well managed it was doubtless the work of this noted gentleman and he seemed to mimic the prisoner in the repetition of the word 'red').

"And that something was found in his possession or he was in such a position that he was about to give the whole thing away ; that is short and——"

"Who says that?" cried the young gentleman, evidently startled, as he glanced quickly and searchingly at the officer, who was about to add, as I supposed, "pointed" or something, "who says I gave a short hand combination ?"

The detective's eyes grew as large as saucers. The prisoner was seized with a most violent fit of coughing.

"Not I," Reynolds remarked, in an innocent off-hand way, "I do not think anybody did."

The prisoner still coughed violently.

"It will be best for you," the detective resumed earnestly, "to make a clean breast of it at once, and the sooner the better; this is your last chance. Do you take it?"

The secretary cast a curious glance at us and I really thought he nodded in acquiescence.

Before I could get my paper out to prepare his statement, I heard the jailer's voice addressed to someone outside the cell-door, saying, "Put them right on that table there."

Speaking to the prisoner he said, "The party is here from the restaurant with your lunch. Will you take it now or wait till these gentlemen retire."

"Oh, certainly, take your lunch at once, sir," I broke in, despite a warning frown from Reynolds, "we will not interrupt you in that interesting pastime, by all means take it now."

I reasoned that we would find the accused in a much more agreeable mood after a substantial meal; and that if he had any intention of making a statement he would be much more confidential over the coffee and cigars.

I was woefully mistaken.

"Red," said the detective, giving him a parting shot as we withdrew to the other side of the room or cell, "is inclined to save himself if he can. But if there is anyone who is to be given the privilege of turning State's evidence and the consequent immunity, you are the man."

I thought I noticed the prisoner's hands trem-
ble while Reynolds was speaking ; it may have
been only imagination on my part.

At all events, if he was at all disconcerted he
recovered at once.

We silently watched him as the jailer and
waiter both busied themselves getting out the
edibles, and if a good appetite is a sign of a
good conscience the private stenographer had
the conscience of an angel.

We drew near when he had about concluded
the substantial portion of the meal.   Then the
waiter spoke through the grating, "Will the
gentleman finish the dessert so that I can remove the dishes ?"

"Certainly," the gentleman answered, and
without another word the lackey handed through
the grating a bottle of wine.

"The boss says that is to keep," he said
and then he passed in a large pie.   This the
warden received, and before handing it over
took up a table knife and ran it around under
the crust.   The steel passed through it easily,
showing that there was no obstruction in its
way.

I surmised that the jailer's action was done
with a view of seeing if there was hidden within
its innocent exterior a knife, file or deadly
weapon.   At all events it attracted our attention
to it.   Apparently satisfied, he laid it before the
prisoner.

I watched the latter when he began at the
dessert, and, he seemed to be in great good
humor as he gingerly broke off a corner of the
rich pastry and began to nibble it.

Reynolds seemed to be in a brown study. He took out his note-book and with his back towards the accused, began to tap it as though testing the point of his pencil.

I noticed several holes made through the upper crust of the pie, evidently with a fork, to let the heat enter or allow the steam, when baking, to escape; and just below these were other holes made with a three-tined fork also, perhaps, indicating the name of the fruit of which it was composed.

You know that all pies look alike, except those in which the generic substance is exposed, such as cranberry, custard and the like. In fact, generally speaking, a pie is like a pudding, the proof is in the eating; though it is a little late for the ordinary citizen to find out what the article is when he has spoiled the sale of it; hence pastry made for restaurants often has its kind indicated as this had..

Well, the accused nibbled at it, drank two glasses of wine, and having lighted a Concha. lolled back in his chair with a quiet, self-satisfied smile on his handsome face.

I felt much encouraged and began where we left off.

"You were about to say that you would make a full, frank and free statement, concerning this matter—in short, give the inside facts of this robbery. Please proceed."

"Sir," he answered coldly, "I said nothing of the kind. If you have any such belief it is entirely without foundation. Nothing has occurred here between us to warrant any such conclusion on your part; quite the contrary."

"You intimated an intention," the detective remarked in a conciliatory tone, " that you would make a clean breast of it."

"Ah," rejoined the other, with a sarcastic smile, "a clean breast of it." "Is this it ?" and he held up the breast bone of a chicken which he had thrown aside, "was that what you referred to ? "

At this I lost my temper and—I don't really know what I did say. The more I ranted and swore the more imperturbable the secretary was. I ended by declaring hotly that it was a childish quibble, a subterfuge, a wriggle, I think I called it ; we would call to-morrow and hoped to find him in a more repentant frame of mind ; I ended by saying that true repentance could not exist without restitution, and if he were still obstinate, information could be had from a more willing source.

I rolled up my still blank paper and we left the prison.

CHAPTER XVII.

THE LAWYER'S STORY. *—Continued.*

MY companion seemed to be considerably displeased as we reached the street.

"I shall certainly throw up the whole case if I am going to be hampered and thwarted by you in this manner," he began. "You may as well understand that first as last."

"Why, what's the matter," I rejoined.

"Matter enough," he answered. "We could have had that statement had it not been for your foolish interference."

"How—when," I interposed, "I certainly did not intend to interfere with you in any way at all."

"Well, doubtless you meant it for the best," he said, somewhat mollified. "But, did you notice that he seemed to be on the point of capitulation just when you suggested that he should have lunch first?" I nodded unconsciously. I certainly thought so.

"Did you see that waiter hand in the wine with the remark that the boss said it was 'to keep'?"

"Yes," I said wonderingly.

"Well, that bottle was labelled 'Mumm,' the signal was as plain as words could make it, Keep Mumm.'"

"Ah!"

"Moreover," he went on, "you heard him

mention or let slip the remark about not having given a short hand combination, when there was no suggestion or thought of the kind, and reasoning by contraries, that is probably just what he did do ; and how he changed when he got at the pie—you saw the upper crust of it full of irregular holes—I took a copy of it as well as I knew how, and I am going to find out if there is anything in it before I am many hours older : This is it."

He quickly took out his note-book and showed me the tapping marks he had made while in the prisoner's cell. I studied it long and carefully.

" There is nothing in that," I said " nothing at all, and nothing in your theory."

" Of course, there may be nothing in it," he replied, "but in the vernacular of criminals, 'peach' means to admit, to inform or confess. I will see what it all means and at once. I have the slips with me and will meet you at your house this evening."

A curt " So long," and he left me, with my thinking cap on and I imagined that there might be just the faintest glimmer of light in the distance.

Before finishing tea that evening he was at the house and informed me that he had had an interview with a party down town who was connected with some court.

" Have your papers and pen ready, I will have a notary and we will take the prisoner's deposition to-morrow at 12 o'clock."

" You speak confidently ; have you found a lever to move the sphinx ? "

"Yes," he answered, "it is right here."

I was all impatience.

"For goodness sake, let me see it."

"You may smile, perhaps, when you see this lever, but I have no doubt of its strength or efficiency."

With these words he opened his coat and took from under his arm two tin plates wrapped in heavy paper and tied tightly face to face with cord. The metal was exposed through an opening in the paper.

This package he proceeded to undo in such a slow, leisurely and methodical way that I almost lost patience. Lifting off one of the plates, finally, he disclosed, what do you suppose? A pie. I repeat it, gentlemen, a pie. Just a plain, every-day, innocent-looking pie.

"Is it loaded or poisoned?" I inquired, thinking the man had taken leave of his senses and it might be just as well to humor him.

"It is not poisoned," he gravely answered, "but I may say it is loaded. At all events, to use your own expression, it is the lever that is to move the sphinx."

He seemed quite sane while saying this, but the thing struck me as so supremely ridiculous that I dropped in a chair and fairly shrieked with laughter. This continued till the tears ran down my cheeks. I managed at last, between bursts of cachination, to say: "The loss of home and friends, the loss of character, coupled with a prospect of twenty years' imprisonment at hard labor are useless to extort an admission of guilt from a prisoner, but it will be done with a pie. Oh, it is too funny for anything," and I went off again.

"When you get through with your idiotic guffaw, I will explain it to you."

His tone was so earnest that I succeeded after a time in recovering composure, and he proceeded with a statement which, though singular, was perhaps plausible.

"After we separated I went down town," he said, " and called on Mr. Schnellschreiber, a personal friend of mine, a stenographer in one of the courts. Having retained him in the case I told him of the wine signal and the prisoner's unguarded statement that he had *not* given a short hand combination. I laid the two papers before him and showed him the *fac simile* of the marks on the pie, which seemed so strengthening to the prisoner when he was about to weaken. This is it :

The first Pie

"After a careful study of it, and, of course, with full knowledge of the circumstances, he intimated, with some degree of positiveness, that it was a communication to the secretary, who was a stenographer, and was just as clear as though it had been in raised letters of gold. It meant 'Do not peach.' This, you see, corroborates my definition as given to you yesterday concerning the word 'peach,' and, taken in connection with the 'keep mum' signal, had a strong tendency to stiffen and strengthen the weak nerves of the prisoner. Do you see it?"

I nodded. It was becoming interesting.

"And Mr. Schnellschrieber suggested that it would be well to try a similar experiment, using another pie with a different inscription. At his direction I procured one, which he signed and sealed, and there it is. What do you think of it?"

It was a very plain pie, yet the thought struck me that there might be something behind it, and I was doing some tall thinking.

Reynolds caught his breath and went on : " I also placed the paper which the officer gave you before him and a copy of the treasurer's combination, and he promised to do his best to cipher something out, and he will meet us here to-morrow at 9 o'clock A. M. I trust you will not allow your desire to giggle to interfere with your preparations for taking the prisoner's deposition at the luncheon hour to-morrow We will bring a notary along."

CHAPTER XVIII.

THE LAWYER'S STORY.—*Continued.*

I CONFESS I was restless, and slept little that night. Try as I would, I could not get the thing out of my mind. At one minute I was inclined to look at the whole thing as a silly fiction of the detective's fertile brain, a fine-spun lot of nonsense, and the next, when I went over it slowly, piece by piece, it did seem somewhat convincing. At all events a few hours would settle it, and we would see what we would see.

Reynolds and his friend Schnellschrieber, the stenographer, were on hand the next morning before I was fully dressed, and while the latter was cooly confident, the former was elated. "It is all right," he whispered. "We have got it dead to rights ; Schnellschrieber is a notary, so you needn't bother about that ; get ready and come on."

He refused to relieve my anxiety by stating further particulars, but bade me possess my soul in patience and wait and see.

The time wore on somehow, and at the hour appointed we reached the prison. Before entering the cell I saw the detective stop and converse earnestly with the jailer. Reynolds gave him something wrapped in a newspaper that looked not unlike a plate, and shook hands with him in a most friendly manner, while we waited for him in the corridor. There he joined us with a very pleasant smile on his face and winked at us as though he had just been appointed to some fat office. We were greeted in the politest manner as we entered the cell by the secretary, and I concluded that this time I should not let my impetuosity disarrange what ever plan the others had in mind, and would allow them to handle the delicate matter in their own way.

The effect of the pie and wine of the previous day was still visible in the imperturbable manner of the prisoner. In addition to his calm politeness he was much more wary and watchful than he had been. He talked of the idiotic charge against him, and referred with some heat to the heavy damages someone would have to pay because of his unjustifiable confinement, and on the whole I felt somewhat over-awed by him.

There was no hint of guilt in his words or actions ; quite the contrary. And I began to surmise, that after all, we were entirely mistaken. The detective did not seem to be much surprised, and the conversation on various subjects proceeded. My paper was still a virgin blank when the jailer announced that lunch was ready, and as the waiter was called away, he would serve it. The meal was handed in, and Slocum did full justice to it. I watched him closely as the detective was remarking: "You will find that the honest way is the shortest and best. There will be no trouble if you will do the right thing in this matter. I told you yesterday that while others might turn State's evidence, it was the desire of your friends that that privilege should be accorded to you in preference to anyone."

The prisoner smiled derisively.

"If you have any doubt about 'Jerry's' inclination we might possibly bring you from parties in a position to know, conclusive proof of it; but it would take time for that, therefore, take my word and——"

"Here is your pie, sir," interrupted the warden. "The wine and cigars the waiter had gone for."

With these words he passed into the cell, and laid down before the prisoner the identical pie which I had seen the night previously in the possession of Reynolds.

The detective winked at me and the prisoner's demeanor changed in a most surprising manner. Never was there such an alteration. The collapse was total and unaccountable. He covered his face with his hands, then looking up suddenly, he said, in a low, faltering tone:

"Well, if the—if a—you get what you ask for; that is, a statement or a—er—you know what I mean—have you entire authority to promise the er—immunity, you speak of?"

"It is useless to beat about the bush longer," the detective answered firmly. "I am authorized to make such promise in behalf of those most interested, if you will do your part and inform us where the securities are. Should you doubt my word, put it in writing; you yourself will go scot free, and there will doubtless be something put in your way to enable you to go where

you can begin life over again. I understand
this is your first false step. You can retrieve
yourself and get in the straight path again. Are
the securities to be had?"

The secretary seemed to be swallowing a
lump in his throat. "I will tell—take this
down," and he began in an almost inaudible
way—"Rather than have others do it, I will
take advantage of your offer."

He proceeded in a slow, hesitating manner,
and finally stated at full length his connection
with the matter, which I reduced to writing. It
is too long to give in detail here.

The all important thing for us was the fact
that the non-negotiable and most of the other
securities were still intact in a tin box at the
office of the Safe Deposit Company, and could
only be had on the strength of a voucher which
he produced.

The substance of his statement was that the
gang took the cash, about $62,000. The securi-
ties were placed in his charge in the belief that
as he knew most about them he could the more
readily convert them, &c.

For over an hour he went right through and
told us the whole business.

It was one of the best planned robberies that
was ever carried through in the metropolis.

The secretary's first false step began at the
race-course where he was a heavy loser. He had
tried to recoup, as so many others have done by
investing what he did not own; he had met
Whang Breaker on the track. Introduction was
followed by intimacy, friendship succeeded intimacy and a proposition to surrender the com-

bination of the strong safe was finally agreed
on.   A scholar like Burchard, the engraver,
counterfeiter and polyglot of the gang, was
thoroughly up in many methods of secret writing, including stenography. The key was agreed
upon and easily mastered by men who have
mastered more profound mysteries.

CHAPTER XIX.

THE LAWYER'S STORY.—*Continued.*

I GOT the sworn statement of the prisoner legally signed, sealed and acknowledged, and the voucher for the securities from the Safe Deposit Company, and after some little delay obtained them. They were securely sealed, endorsed: "To be delivered on presentation of the voucher."

As the box afterward showed there were over $700,000 worth of paper, railroad stocks and bonds, notes, certificates of indebtedness, bonds and mortgages, &c.

Great as my hurry was to handle the securities I waited long enough to take a careful inspection of that miraculous pie.

I broke off a corner, tasted it and still lived. While on our way for the securities, Schnellschrieber explained it. It was punched with a fork in this manner:

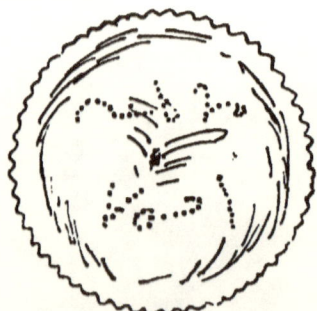

A Pie with another inscription.

As translated for me it said: "Make best terms, Jerry has given up."

It was only a pie, but "when the pie was opened the bird began to sing."

CHAPTER XX.

THE LAWYER'S STORY.—*Continued.*

WELL, I got the tin box and brought it to the Southampton Trust Company, and, you may be sure there was a genuine love feast among the sedate old trustees when we got there with the valuables.

The detective was hugged and kissed by those grey-headed old fellows in a way that was shameful and almost wanton.

While this mutual admiration society was in session there was an elaborate feast—"a spread," Reynolds called it—prepared and served in the president's room. Then we had speeches, toasts, &c.,—I was referred to as the most clever anything, and Reynolds was promised enough to make him rich for the rest of his life.

Amid breathless silence Schnellschrieber was called upon and explained the whole cipher. He found it out by the merest chance, he said, although no one believed this : " I saw the words ' stenography' reversed after ' 4th,' and happening then to look at the other paper, I observed that it said " short hand upside down," and that to be sure is plain enough. It was by the merest chance I discovered that and the rest was easy. A child could see through it. This is the whole thing as plain as a pike-staff.

"Put the burglar's 'key' in short hand characters according to any of the modern systems of swift writing, 'write and reverse' the burglar's key and you have the treasurer's key.

```
To open safe
1st·   Outside nick between D & 4
2nd·   Inner notch at 11
3rd·   Long hand to 6 twice
4th·   Shorthand upside down
       W· M· M· Treasurer·
```

"In order that you may understand, I now put these scraps in juxtaposition.

"First: the one spoken of as the 'Treasurer's Key.' Immediately below it is the paper known as the 'Burglar's Key.'

"On the upper margin of this, as I am informed, appeared originally a small piece of plaster, containing the words 'this over fine,' but being exceedingly frail or fragile, it had crumbled into dust. A copy of the writing was made, and

```
All plo ways
1st; Destroy Mike, may not be
6lients: Man Jim | fresh
Thinned; Madam 2.62. snout
4th:     Studerouers
   - Seven or a tire
     except - - - - -
```

no particular care was exercised to preserve the plaster containing the simple words, even if it were possible, which I very much doubt.

"At all events, the portion referred to did not make a complete sentence, and while we do not know just what preceded the word 'this,' we can easily imagine that the meaning was a direction or caution.

"Glancing at these scraps in close proximity, the professional eye will readily discern that the 'Burglar's Key' is the 'Treasurer's Key.'

"This is manifest. Here it is in stenographic characters :

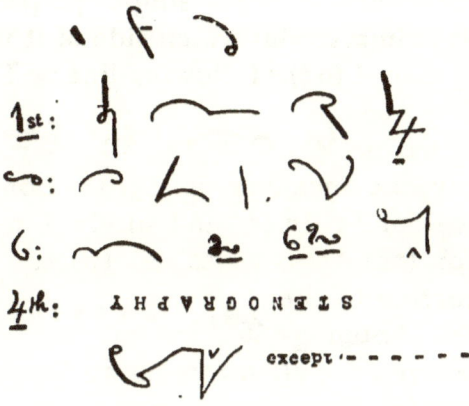

1st:

ω:

6:

4th: STENOGRAPHY

except ᐟ - - - - -

"I reverse this sheet now and read from the right to the left *except* as the cipher states plainly the figures with dashes under them, as - - - - - - six of them.

"To make it more explicit let us take it in sections: 'All Plo ways' with the stenographic characters, I invert the page, vowellize it, and the reading is, 'To open Safe.'

"The next line is: 1st, Destroy Mike, may not be with" the proper short hand written:

"Inverted and read towards the left; it indicates plainly : 'Outside nick between D & 4.'

"The '1st' and '4th' come under the exception stated and have short dashes beneath them.

"We recur to the next line. It begins, as you perceive, 'Clients ; Man Jim at fresh,' putting this in stenographic characters revers-ing and reading the transcription is '2d: Inner notch at 11.'   The 'at' is made by the short hand 't' a recognized 'sign word,' and being a single perpendicular stroke, it is immaterial which side of it is up.

"We proceed to the following line : 'Thinned, madam 2 62 snout ;' that is Obviously, the meaning is '3rd : Long hand to 6 twice' or '2 times,' and surely I need not say to you that 'two times' is 'twice.'

"Recurring to the last line; 'Stenography' as you are all aware is an interchangeable word for 'short hand,' and when one sees the sign stenography reversed or inverted in this manner: Λ૧ԁɐɹɓouǝʇS, he knows without further explanation that it is 'short hand' upside down.

Finally, 'seven or a tire' is like this and if you understood ever so little about any of the systems of swift writing you would perceive at a glance when you turned the paper and looked at this that it was the key to the whole thing. It is 'write and reverse,' with the exceptions stated. That's all. The entire thing is really elementary, but like many other very simple things you don't comprehend the great simplicity of it till you understand it.

"Doubtless the words on the wall were, 'Study this over fine' or 'con' or 'read' or some such thing, so that when they got through the wall they just opened the safe at once. It follows that the safe expert's report was correct and the police theory all wrong.

"It is quite ingenious and was fairly well executed.

"After all you have not lost so much, every-thing is lovely, and here is to us all."

I remember while the applause evoked by Schnellscrieber's clever explanation was at its height I thought of the lonely days of James in prison, the dead janitor, the widow and children, and I am sure some such thought came into Mr. Ames' mind, for I noticed him putting down names and figures on a slip of paper for some good purpose, I know.

Well, we had what the detective called "a humming old time."

I myself got pretty well for the one time in my life. The last thing I remember seeing was the treasurer and Jim, the Janitor, waltzing around, while half a dozen venerable looking directors were "patting Juba."

CHAPTER XXI.

THE LAWYER'S STORY.—*Continued.*

THIS most gigantic robbery dwindled down to a loss of less than $70,000.

I subsequently made it my business to get a thousand dollars from the bank officials and in less than forty-eight hours I slipped it into Slocum's hands as I bade him good-bye at the door of the city prison. There was no proof against him and he was discharged as a matter of course. I have not seen him since but I have heard indirectly that he is an honest man in a distant city, and has succeeded in retrieving his one false step.

The other parties were never discovered—in fact, we didn't look for them and don't want them any more; they got over $60,000. They can keep it and keep themselves away.

The reader paused.

"And is that all," said the Host?

"No" said the Lawyer, as the smile faded from his face and his voice faltered; "no," he said softly. "Some balmy spring day you may perchance enter a cemetery not many miles from this great bustling city; you pass along the broad gravelled carriage drive where the air is laden with the odor of flowers. You see many mounds with great white shafts above them, and many humbler graves marked only with the soft verdure that nature plants on God's acre.

"Passing through the winding walks of the City of the Dead you at length come to a corner obscure and alone.   You see a mound there. Above it a great grey boulder.   Behind the stone a small weeping willow tree droops gracefully over the unhewn rock, its slender branches sway and bend in the gentle breeze and almost hide the stone from view.

" There is a brass plate on the southerly corner of the rock, with the inscription, 'Erected by the Officers and Trustees of the Southampton Trust Company,' and a long reference to the quiet sleeper beneath the mound.

"Go closer; bend low, and lift the swaying branches from the face of the stone, and you see deeply cut in its rugged front :

In Memory
of
Michael.
'Faithful unto Death.' "

The Lawyer turned his back to the company and blew his nose loudly ; the Coroner had his hand over his face, apparently asleep, though his lips were quivering ; the Host seemed to be taking motes from his eyes with the corner of his handkerchief ; the Stenographer was intently studying the pattern of the carpet, and the Real Estate Man was silently staring through the window at the dismal darkness of the winter's night.

The silence was unbroken, save for an occasional sniff, low and sob-like.

They were men of many callings, varying creeds and different nationalities, but, "One touch of Nature makes the whole world kin."

CHAPTER XXII.

THE PRISONER'S NOTES.

THE worshipers were promptly gathered at
the shrine.

It being understood that on this evening it
was the Real Estate Man's turn to " shoot off his
mouth," as the Host expressed it, the other members were filled with curiosity to see how the
poor gentleman would acquit himself.

The worshipers were promptly gathered at the shrine.

After many apologies about a severe cold,
which rendered him very hoarse, about the lack
of opportunity for preparation, and a piteous
appeal for an extension of time, that was promptly voted down, the sufferer adjusted his glasses

at the proper angle, produced a great coil of paper, which, amid the profound silence of the company, he unrolled, and, having taken the kink out, read as follows :

An isolated, bleak, desolate place. Never inviting, it is gloomy, if not uncanny looking on this dark, cheerless November day.

A barren spot indeed, as may be known by the stunted cedars and scrub oaks that strive to get sustenance from the hard, stony ground. No sunlight seems to strike it. No birds are carolling blithely from leafy trees.

No sound, save ever and anon a faint shriek of unearthly laughter, and the almost inaudible but steady "clink, clink," of hammering stone. Around about you all is desolate, grim, cheerless.

In the background stand a group of great stone buildings, surrounded by massive walls. The sinister and forbidding appearance of the nearest structure is intensified by a glance at the iron-latticed windows, through the interstices of which are seen pale, drawn faces—faces that, once seen, are not forgotten in many a day. Gaunt, wolfish, terror-stricken, white, with glaring eyes ; some tear-stained and intelligent looking, but all bearing in some respect the awful mark of God's greatest affliction—a shattered mind.

Just beyond is another structure. They are both public institutions.

In one it sometimes happens that iniquity, under the guise of charity, does its hideous work. And despite the power of riches, some of the patients here are wealthy.

The poor are not so often declared insane, without sufficient excuse. Having no estates, there is no good reason why they should be. Without relatives financially interested in their incarceration, the very poor, even when somewhat demented, are suffered to plod along in the even tenor of their way, oblivious of certificates signed by experts, unclutched by the grip of the modern press-gang, and live out their little lives, enjoying liberty and the pursuit of happiness——"

The Coroner interrupted the reader :

" Excuse me for breaking in here, but a thought strikes me——"

The aggravating Host interrupted in turn, in a tone of feigned interest :

" Oh, how singular ! Strike you hard, and where ? "

" It is this," said the little Irishman, heedless of the Host : "The wisdom exhibited by the Fathers, when they declared that every man had the right to life, liberty, and the pursuit of happiness. You observe it is the *pursuit*, not the possession, and people have been pursuing it for thousands of years—will pursue it to the end and can never grasp it, so that it may be true after all that men must first 'seek the kingdom of God,' that the other things may be added. And it seems to me that Moore put it gloriously when he said :

> " This world is all a fleeting show,
>   For man's illusion given ;
> The smiles of Joy, the tears of Woe,
> Deceitful shine, deceitful flow—
>   There's nothing true but Heaven.'

"But," began the sarcastic gentleman, "where do you put the narratives we have been listening to, and the men——"

"Order, order!" the Lawyer said, authoritatively, " we are here to listen to a story, and these discussions are entirely inappropriate and uncalled for."

The irrepressible gentleman was not to be subdued.

" Why, I have heard it said by good authority, that men would be happy but they want too much. There *is* happiness. The truest and most perfect picture of happiness and contentment that I ever saw was a hog that lay grunting in three feet of soft mud, and I have seen a cow in a meadow chewing its cud——pray, excuse me," he said abruptly, as the Real Estate Man with a look of displeasure on his face began to fold up his papers—" Pray excuse me and proceed."

The reader resumed :

Let us enter this sepulchre—we may justly call it such, for although the inmates have physical life in their bodies, yet, they are in reality dead to the world. What matters to them progress in the arts and sciences ; like the brutes of the field and the birds of the air they have no thought but to eat, to drink, to sleep.

Grasping the strong balustrade, we go up the broad staircase to the big door with its massive hinges, tremendous knob, double panels and solid stiles which seem to say that all may not pass here. We pull the bell at the door frame and a deep, resonant clang, reverberates through the long halls of the madhouse. After some delay there is a noise of the unloosening of bolts, the door opens a few inches, and a grizzly, strongly marked face peers through the aperture: "You can't come in here. Visitors' day is next month.—Oh, a pass from the superintendent? Come." Another moment, the chain is off and the big door swings open. After presenting the proper voucher you are directed to follow the keeper and pass through the long, clean corridors, now silent and deserted. The inmates are at dinner. Everywhere, cleanliness and order.

I digress here long enough to challenge the truth of the two old saws that "Cleanliness is next to Godliness," and that "Order is heaven's first law." One is merely the trade-mark of some wide-awake soap maker, and while the other rests on fair authority, it is none the less false. You see at a glance that order reigns here. And order reigned in Warsaw after the devastating armies passed over it and crushed the people; then there was order, for there was no life to create disorder.

The resident superintendent, as he smilingly bids you welcome, warns you that, "It is one of the singular idiosyncracies of nearly all forms of dementia known to alienists that the more the unfortunates insist upon their complete sanity the more unbalanced they are; and, it not unfrequently happens that visitors to such institutions, who are otherwise intelligent, after the round of inspection, go forth with a strong impression, if not a preposterous belief, that sane persons are sometimes under confinement as demented, and that the innocent often suffer the

punishment of the guilty. This never occurs.
Never. There is scarce room for the unquestionably insane, and no innocent person is ever
unjustly confined. Reilly, show the gentlemen
through the male ward and prison."

Following the attendant into the almost empty
wards, and then to the grounds, we see the sad-
dest sights that the human eye has ever beheld.

The most incongruous companionship is observed in the scattered groups about the court-
yard. In one corner two very aged gentlemen
and a mere boy are playing some childish game
with small stones. Here a native American and
an unmistakable Briton with clasped hands are
sauntering lovingly up and down the yard.
There an Irishman and an Israelite sit on one
bench with arms entwined in reverential affection. Another loving group, partly French,
partly German, in a corner of the enclosure indicates that the ordinary feelings of sane men
have no place in this remote retreat. Other
sights there are, strange, heart-rending and
gruesome. We forbear to describe them, or the
chatter of those who imagine themselves to be
kings, emperors, popes and potentates possessing
unlimited wealth and innumerable slaves to carry
out their wishes. We follow the guide to a
break in the otherwise solid wall. He inserts a
key in an iron door, pushes us through the opening, quickly turns and secures the door. This is
the outer yard of the prison. Through another
higher and stone-capped wall and we are within
the inner enclosure in which the jail proper is
situated. Cheerless and forbidding as this great
grey structure is, it is less gloomy than the build-

ing we have just left. One of these buildings is
the frying pan ; the other is the fire. The term
of confinement in one is fixed by law. The
term of incarceration in the other depends upon
the mental condition of the subject. In one the
demented ; in the other the malefactor. In one
idiocy and indifference darken the countenance
of the inmate ; in the other the expectation of
release brightens the face of the criminal. In
one the incarcerated bear the mark of mental
affliction ; in the other Hope brightens days to
come.

The heavily ironed door that leads to the
first tier of cells in this building bears on its
lintel a sign as of mockery : "The way of the
transgressor is hard." As if these poor creatures
knew it not ! It is thrust on the attention of
even the most callous every minute, of every
hour, of every day in the long and weary years
of their confinement "at hard labor." Aye!
even until the iron grip of the law in due course
of time is relaxed, the clemency of the execu-
tive is moved to intervene, or, until "The night
cometh and no man can work." Yes, "the way
of the transgressor *is* hard."

The strong walls grimly frown it. The
furtive looks show it. The ironed barred windows bespeak it. The ball and chain strike it
as they come together. The great metal door
emphasizes it in every clang. The air that fil-
ters through the little high windows whispers it.
The hard-faced jailers jingle it in the rattle of
the big keys. The handcuffs click it. The
dark cell, the solitary confinement, the coarse
fare, all—all tell the unfortunate in unmistak-

able tones and without the aid of the emblazon-
ed sign on the outer walls that, "The way of
the transgressor *is* hard."

As you stand here the prisoners come from
the dining-room, rapidly and in disorderly
squads.

Joe

"Halt!" comes from a keeper· in a harsh
voice. "Form and fall in; drop the left hand
to your sides; put-your-right hand-on-the-right-
shoulder-of-the-man-in-front. Steady, now.
Shuffle."

It is the "lock step," executed with military
precision, and the men are going out to break

stone for the State.   No laughing, no pushing.
Every man falls into his place.

A mere boy, intelligent and innocent looking,
tries in vain to catch the eyes of the visitors. A
warning shout from a keeper, and with averted
face, he passes on with his fellows.   At a little
distance the close, compact, moving mass of human beings in the striped garb, looks not unlike
a great spotted serpent winding its way through
the huge gateway.   After a time the strangers
follow the gang to watch the work.

Again the youthful prisoner endeavors to attract the notice of the obtuse visitors, but a loud
imprecation from the watchful keeper warns
him that the infraction will be punished.

Tiring of the monotony, heart sick of the
whole thing, the stupid visitors wait but a moment and depart.   Like the Idols of the Gen-
tiles, having eyes, they see not.   They fail to
note the agony of the boyish face, the furtive
attempts to attract their attention, the awful
desire to speak.

At the risk of punishment—the coarse bread,
the impure water, the dark cell, he is about to
put his idea into execution.   He fears not his
fate too much, but will put it to the touch at all
hazards, and he rises.

Too late ! they are gone.   Too late !   Again ?
"How long, O, Lord, how long ?"   And again
as before the tears drop hot and fast on the
hardened stone and melt it not.   Nor have they
softened the hearts of jailers.   He is young,
buoyant, hopeful, and even as the bitter tears
blind him he thinks in his heart, "Blessed are

they who hunger and thirst after justice, for they shall be filled."

Many months afterwards one of the visitors learned the facts embodied in this additional manuscript, which I may call the sequel to this prelude.

The boyish prisoner was not baffled in the end.

He mourned and was comforted. He suffered persecution for Justice's sake, and came to his kingdom after all.

The relation concerns him, and begins in this way.

CHAPTER XXIII.

IT was a very ordinary looking dwelling-house in a thriving town in ——

Its look of plainness was increased by the drawn shutters, and the almost uninhabited look of the whole exterior, for the windows and doors were shut close.

No shout of children playing in the yard broke the solemn stillness. No sign of house-work was to be seen.

At rare intervals a villager entered at the dilapidated gate-way, passed through the yard to the rear of the house, walked noiselessly in and spoke in whispers.

The black crape streaming from the knob of the door told the sad story. There was death in the house.

No wonder that the passer-by sighed. No wonder that the good women wept and spoke softly.

Death was present in its worst form. In the humble, darkened sitting-room, resting on two chairs, was a cheap stained coffin containing all that remained of the dead woman, aged, as the cheap plate put it " 32 years."

Around about the casket sat a few neighbors and the bereaved children—a little girl and two boys, aged respectively, four, eleven and four-teen.

All were silent, save when a mournful wail or

a barely suppressed sob broke the stillness of the room.

The father and husband sat at the head of the coffin apparently stunned and disheartened. There was a look of sleeplessness, of fatigue, and a faint indication of dissipation or indecision, on his strongly ·marked and weather-beatenface.

John Morley and his wife Ann, had- started life hand in hand some fifteen years before, with good health and nothing else. God had blessed their union with three children.

The boys attended school in a near-by city, Joseph, the eldest, being of a studious turn of mind had been encouraged to learn phonography with other branches of knowledge. The boys had been progressing fairly well at school, but, since the mother's grievous illness, household matters had not gone just as they should have. Minnie, the girl, was a mere babe. Although the elder children did their utmost to assist in the household work and to continue their studies, it was found difficult to retain the usual orderly routine. One of the boys was required to be in constant attendance at his mother's bedside, and cleanliness, order, and promptness, in serving the meals was the exception. During his wife's illness the father began gradually to neglect his home.

Occasionally, too, he came home from the shop with a sleepy, watery look about the eyes, walking with unsteady gait and speaking with thick utterance. The truth is the man was unstable and weak. The ailing condition of his wife and the almost helpless condition of the family, instead of making him stand firm and equal to the emergency, discouraged and disheartened him.

The dying wife saw that he was failing in his duties, but alas, was powerless to prevent it. He disliked to remain at home in the evenings. He could not bear it, he said, it was not a man's place; let the children or the neighbors do that; he could do her no good.

The woman's sickness, consumption, had the usual termination. After long suffering that she bore like a martyr, her spirit went to God.

The thin worn hands were folded across the dead woman's breast; the simple shroud was wrapped about the wasted form and the freshly upturned earth in the cemetery told the end.

The little family vainly struggled to recover from the shock. The father made weak attempts in his own poor way to conduct household matters properly, but after a few signal failures, gave it up.

Gradually, he absented himself from home. Night after night he spent at the public house or visiting the neighbors. Thus he soon forgot his bereavement.

Matters went on in this way for several months. At length Morley married again. The new Mrs. Morley although neither comely nor in the prime of life, had what was said to be important to Morley : an interest in some farming land supposed to be valuable.

After her advent, household affairs, formerly barely tolerable, became decidedly unpleasant. A woman of ungovernable temper, from the first she seemed to have an intense dislike to her

husband's children, and took every occasion to
manifest it.   Looking upon them as interlopers.
on the slightest provocation, even without excuse, she scolded, insulted, and chastised them
severely.   Little mementoes of the dead woman
hoarded as treasures, she disdainfully threw in
the dust heap despite the tears and protests of
the children.   Under this treatment they became
restive.   Complaints to the father brought
neither redress nor interference, and served
only to increase the wife's anger.   This state of
things gradually made the children cross and
peevish.   It was a house divided against itself,
and could not stand.   Bickering was not uncommon.   The elder lad seemed to come in for
a large share of unreasonable abuse ; and the
once quiet boy answered the stepmother with
disrespect and anger.   She said and did what
most aggravated him.   Again and again appeals
were made to the father.   A weak protest on
his part was followed by prompt submission,
"Anything for peace sake," he said.

CHAPTER XXIV.

ONCE after the boys had gone to school, noting the absence of the little girl, her stepmother called her impatiently. There was no immediate response. The woman softly crept up the garret stairs, and finding the child, she roughly accused her of heedlessness and seizing a stout billet of wood was about to inflict condign punishment on her.

Just then the elder boy returning, entered the house. At the sight of his sister, pale and trembling and the passion distorted face of the woman, he unfortunately gave way to anger. All the real and fancied insults and ill-treatment he had suffered, came to his mind and his blood boiled.

"Let my sister alone," he cried, and he rushed to the rescue. His only intention was to protect the girl. In striving to save the child a disgraceful hand-to-hand struggle ensued. In scuffling about the enraged woman tripped on some obstacle, and in falling heavily to the floor struck her head against the stove. At that instant, a peddler, who had been a silent witness of the occurrence from the open door-way, seeing the unpleasant termination of the affair, uttered a loud cry and rapidly left the scene. The woman lay gasping and unconscious with the blood slowly oozing from a dreadful wound in the head.　The boy retained the weapon from which she had released her grasp and for a brief instant he stood over the bleeding woman in this guilty attitude.　Save for the presence of the injured woman, he was alone.　Early in the struggle, the little girl had run out shrieking.　Her cries and the noise of the struggle brought the neighbors into the room and they observed the lad in the compromising position referred to.

Scarcely knowing what he said Joe uttered a loud cry of "What have I done?" and stooping down attempted to raise the woman's head on his lap.

To his intense horror, she was gasping.　Another moment, and she was dead.　The limbs were rapidly growing stiff and cold.　The dead eyes glared at him.　Neighbors gathered about uttering wild cries of consternation and affright. Shocked as they were, no pen or tongue can describe the speechless, ghastly terror of the lad. Deprived of reason and almost of utterance, by the awful occurrence he jabbered some incoherent excuse, while those who had heard his words and the noise of the struggle and saw the blood-stained weapon in his hand, looked at him askance and shook their heads.

Stunned and shocked by the awful accident— unconscious of the dreadful predicament in which he was placed, the dazed youth could say nothing in his own behalf.　Circumstances were strongly against him. ` He was discovered red-handed, the horror of guilt on his face.

The local police took the necessary steps, and acted throughout the dreadful proceeding on the only apparent theory—guilt.　Of course, the ill-feeling between the dead woman and the step-son was known. It was believed by all that the woman had undertaken to chastise the little girl, this was forcibly resented by Joe, and unfortunately, allowing his temper to overcome his reason, he had struck the woman and wounded her to death. It was too plain. The accused did not deny it. He could not. Had he done so, the denial would not be accepted in the face of the circumstantial evidence. The most that could be said was that he did not mean murder; the blow was unintentionally severe, perhaps. Yet he was none the less guilty of bloodshed.

But barely charitable as this construction was it was entertained by few or none. The distracted father appeared on the scene crying for vengeance before he knew the facts, and the boy was soon lodged in jail on a charge of Murder.

The county court of ―― was in session and the case was promptly disposed of. The Jury found a verdict of murder against the boy with a recommendation to mercy on account of his youth and previous good character.

The accused was sentenced to fifteen years at hard labor in prison. There was no interference on his behalf by anyone; his friends turned from him for the reason that his natural protector believed him guilty, and the father certainly did not oppose any obstacle to the due course of law. Within a few days after the trial the sheriff of the county, with a commitment under the seal of the court appeared on the scene, and by him the poor lad was placed in the bleak and gloomy prison that I have attempted to describe in the opening of this story, and had for his close companions, some of the most incorrigible of the criminal classes.

It so happened that one of the keepers in charge of the stone-breaking gang in which the lad was placed in jail, was distantly related to the deceased woman, and this man's feelings were decidedly hostile to the boy.

This is hardly to be wondered at ; he believed as the jury did, that the young convict was a red-handed murderer, who had escaped gallows by a technicality. No sooner was the youthful prisoner within his power than he began a course of treatment towards him, both in regard to the day's task and infractions of the prison rules that made Joe's life in the institution seem like a hideous nightmare.

CHAPTER XXV.

THE prisoner after a time seemed to have recovered his senses, so to speak; he could look
back now with reasonable composure at the
horrid scene in which he had been a participant,
and for which he had suffered so grieviously.
He began to think that if the trial were to take
place again, he could have convinced the jury
that he was entirely innocent. He remembered
now that the peddler had seen the occurrence,
and while he did not know where the man could
be found, he felt that if he could be produced,
his evidence would be sufficient for an acquittal.
He vainly attempted to communicate with those
who were or should have been his friends. No
letters were allowed to go from prisoners unless
with the sanction and concurrence of the prison
authorities. No communication passed from the
convict to the outside world save such as suited
the prison officials. Letters were sent and intercepted. Smarting under a sense of injustice,
weak from lack of proper food, worrying about
the condition of his brother and sister from
whom he was entirely isolated, coupled with
thoughts of his own forlorn and friendless state
made his lot anything but enviable. He wrote
a kind and truthful letter to his father in which
he spoke of his sad life in the prison, and begged
him " for God's sake " to hunt up the one witness of the dreadful occurrence, whose truthful

statement, he had no doubt, would fully exoner-
ate him, adding, that he would either die or go
mad if his afflictions in the prison continued. It
was piteous but useless. The letter was opened
in the main office by one of the officials who informed the convict that they did not allow such
reports of ill-treatment to be made by prisoners,
so tenderly cared for by the merciful authorities
of the jail. Again and again he strove to communicate with visitors.

This was an infraction always punished. He
endeavored to send word through the discharged prisoners—to those he thought might be-
friend him, his schoolmates, his mother's relatives, his teachers, but no one cared to interfere
in his behalf.

Placed in jail under circumstances that seemed
to justify it, his own father and neighbors being
the principal witnesses against him, those who
would otherwise have interfered held aloof, fearing that it might be meddling in family affairs
which did not concern them.

The only letter it was permissible to send
from the prison was one expressing gratitude to
those in charge of the institution, extolling the
management, and praising the officials for their
thoughtful consideration of those under their
charge. All communications, which in the
slightest degree commented on or criticised the
prison management were intercepted or destroyed, or returned to the prisoner with a reprimand
and occasionally something more. So it is not
surprising that no letter was received from the
boy during the long period of his incarceration,
certainly none that would cause uneasiness

among friends, if there were any who desired to aid him.

One day in each month was set apart for visitors, and although poor Joe had no friends to call upon him, he was carefully removed on these occasions from the sight of callers to a lonely cell.

The annual visit of inspection by the State Prison Authorities was to be made to the jail on the 29th of May. Although conversation was strictly prohibited among the prisoners, this fact leaked out and Joe hoped much from it.

The unfortunate lad's hope was that he would have an opportunity of stating his case to some of the humane public authorities, who would look into it and do justice for justice's sake.

Judge of his dismay, when informed that during the time of the visit of inspection, he was to be placed in a remote part of the institution where he could neither see nor communicate with the visitors. Early on the morning set apart for the inspection, he was ordered to throw the loose paving stones that had been trimmed by the prisoners from the gravel walk to the side of the road, so as to allow the carriages of the officials free access through the prison yard.

This work was to be completed by ten o'clock, the visitors being due at eleven. While engaged in this task a bright idea occurred to the lad which he thought it well to put into practice. Although the keen eyes of the keeper were upon him, he managed in carrying the stones to place them on the hill-side in this order:

"There," thought the boy, "thanks to my education I have been able to do that. If the overseer understands it I may spend years in

this place ; if he does not it will be strange indeed, if some of the visitors do not see and
comprehend it."

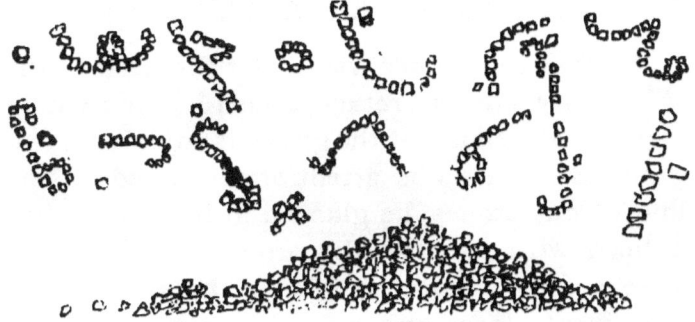

He was ordered back to his cell, and shortly
afterwards the Inspector and the Governor's
Secretary, accompanied by a party of ladies and
gentlemen, entered the prison yard. The Inspector, followed by his wife and little boy, mounted
the staircase on one side of the prison yard and
admirably performed the duty of watching the
prisoners file before him under the care of the
keeper, after which he shook hands with the
prison authorities, congratulated the prisoners
on their happy life, advising them to be good,
and just, and fear not, etc., and finished the inspection by eating a good dinner at the expense
of the State.

CHAPTER XXVI.

WHILE the dinner was under discussion, the Governor's secretary, a keen-looking young man, sauntered about the grounds enjoying a fragrant Havana. His attention attracted to the pile of cut stones, he glanced at it casually and noticed with surprise the order in which they were placed. Another glance, he rubbed his eyes, went closer and looked again. Then he uttered a low whistle.

"Well," he said, when he had somewhat recovered, "this is most remarkable; it cannot be an accident; it is surely a singular thing. I will see about it."

He was about to call the attention of one of the keepers to what he had first thought might be an odd coincidence or whim of a prisoner, but paused. The mere fact that these stones were placed in such an order, indicated to him that if they were placed there by design, the person who so placed them desired secrecy, for some reason.

"It can do no harm," thought the secretary, "to carry out the party's intention, for the present, at least."

While these thoughts were passing through his mind, he re-read the characters, slowly, carefully, and without difficulty :

"An innocent boy is being ill-treated in this place and cannot complain. Help! Cell 10. Joe."

"It spells that," said the secretary, softly, "if it spells anything, and while they are finishing dinner I will see it through."

Taking out a slip of paper he carefully noted the number of the cell, as indicated by the stones, and continued his walk towards the rear of the prison. The young man was wise beyond his years, and thought it well not to be too abrupt in seeking knowledge.

"Which are the even-numbered cells?" he asked of the keeper. The latter bowed respectfully and obsequiously as he indicated the tier of cells on the east side of the building.

"Ah," said the secretary, "where is the inmate of number eight?"

On being informed by the keeper that the prisoner referred to was in the hospital, the secretary said :

"Well, suppose you send me number ten?"

"Certainly," answered the keeper, hesitatingly, "but he's a bad one."

"No matter about that," retorted the secretary, authoritatively, "that's just the kind of a one that I want."

In five minutes more Joe was tearing out like a madman, in advance of the keeper. With sobs and tears he began, in a disconnected and incoherent way, to tell his sad story. By degrees the clever young secretary put the lad at his ease and got possession of the essential facts of the case, which he promised to lay before the governor.

At his suggestion the peddler was hunted up by clever detectives, sent down from the metropolis, and the man's statement, under oath, together with the boy's previous good character, counted for something. Above all, the testimony of a clever doctor, who had attended the deceased woman for a number of years, to the effect that the dead woman was subject to heart disease, and that the position and condition of the wound, as described before the coroner's jury, could not possibly have caused her death, was procured.

This brightened the outlook, and a little of the sunshine penetrated the gloomy recesses of the jail. There was a revulsion of public feeling. Newspapers vied with each other in publishing accounts of it, under startling headlines :

" The Clever Ruse of an Innocent Youth," " Justice Triumphant," etc.

Nothing succeeds like success. The jailers, once exacting, harsh and tyrannical, became polite, considerate and almost servile to the once oppressed victim, and, in less than a month, the re-habilitated convict stood on the outside of the great grim door, unfettered, basking in the sunlight of freedom, unshackled ; free.

Good fortune continued with him. His benefactor stood by him manfully. The once friendless lad, before whom the future had looked so dark ; the wearer of the striped suit, who bid fair to become a dangerous member of society, is now, thanks to knowledge and kindness, a rising man in the office of his firm friend, in the city of ——

The reader paused, with a sign of satisfaction, and carelessly crammed the manuscript into the coal scuttle.

" Well," said the Host, " it ends well, don't it ?

If ever that young man gets tired of that position, I shall be glad to introduce him to the
Coroner here, who may want another clerk——"

Without waiting for further sarcasms, a motion to adjourn was promptly put by the Coroner, and as promptly carried by a majority, and
the Host was left alone to address his conclud-
ing remarks to the smouldering embers in the
grate.

CHAPTER XXVII.

THE TRAMP STENOGRAPHER.

THE parties met by appointment. All were present but the Stenographer. As that gen-

The Victim of Circumstances.

tleman was usually prompt his continued absence excited comment, if not uneasiness. While the members present were still discussing the probable cause of his absence and considering the advisability of adjourning there was a knock at the door and the missing gentleman came in,

He was not alone. In his wake was an exceedingly seedy individual who slouched into an obscure corner of the room in a fruitless endeavor to make himself as unconspicuous as possible. The person will bear a brief description. The shabby dress coat that enveloped his person was closely buttoned about his throat with the evident design of hiding the absence or unlaundried condition of a collar or perhaps a larger garment of wearing apparel.

The man was about forty years of age and had perhaps a week's growth of hair on his face. He was dressed in odds and ends of clothing, the individual contributions of the charitably disposed. Clad in a fat man's trousers, a boy's waistcoat, a slender gentleman's coat, he wore a pair, or what was left of a pair, of lady's shoes, much dilapidated, in the condition known as "down at the heels." A soft hat sat at a raking angle on his, by no means unintellectual looking head.

This weather beaten headgear he removed and exhibited an exceedingly unkempt head of hair. He was an odd and singular looking person, but the man carried himself well, in fact jauntily, despite his poor attire and rather rough appearance.

Apparently in the first stage of consumption, the only sanative indication about him was a nose with a real healthy, ruddy, "countrified" look. Flanking this member was a pair of bright grey eyes, and below a mouth with just the least hint of a smile lurking in its corners. There was about the fellow a certain "style"— a combination of dirt and dignity difficult to un-

derstand and impossible to describe. As before
stated, he shuffled to a corner of the room behind
a chair in the endeavor to make himself as unobserved as possible. This intention was abruptly frustrated by the Stenographer who took
the stranger's hand and drawing the reluctant
individual towards the middle of the room introduced him as a friend and fellow-craftsman,
adding: "The night is cold, he is not overclad,
and if you have anything at hand for such cases,
made and provided, trot it out." The Host
soon placed a pitcher of beer on the table with
the necessary utensils. Without a word the
visitor pushed the poker in the open fire, filled
a glass and having darkened the white froth
with a good sprinkling of pepper he plunged
the red hot iron into the chilled ale. With a
cheerful sniff at the ascending steam a glance at
the company and a "God bless us all, gentlemen," the stranger lifted the glass to his lips
and put the mulled bumper where he believed
it would do the most good. A second and a
third followed in rapid succession. Then the
stranger turned to the company, a different man
in his own estimation, and the others observed
with surprise that he seemed to have lost the re-
served "slouchy" look before so conspicuous.

Bowing to the company, he said by way of
introduction "You see before you, gentlemen,
one who is called by a cold and heartless world,
'tramp.' I am the victim of circumstances."

"Quite so," murmured the quiet gentleman.

The Stenographer spoke up: "I met this gentleman under peculiar circumstances. As you
perceive, he is a man, and as such has a claim

on us all, for we are all brothers in Adam.   As
a fellow-craftsman of mine he has an especial
claim on me ; in addition to this he has also an
especial claim on you, gentlemen, for I was attracted to him by his truthfulness and no one
knows better than I, your great appreciation of
that sublime virtue."

"Explain this mystery, for goodness sake,"
said the Coroner, in a quick, jerky way, "Let
us have it."

"I stood on the street a few minutes since,"
the scribe began, "conversing with a friend ; I
facing the roadway and my friend facing me.
Suddenly I heard a voice saying, 'Say, boss,
would you mind giving a fellow a lift ?'   My
friend, who was addressed by the gentleman
now present, looked up with the curt remark,
'Ah, you want a lift ; that is a quarter ; and I
know just what you want it for.   Your wife is
dying on the upper floor of a tenement house
and you need a little money to get medicine that
may preserve her life or some little thing to
cool the parched tongue of the dying woman,
Eh ?' 'No,' said the stranger, smilingly, 'No,
boss, that ain't it.' 'Oh,' said my friend, somewhat surprised, 'I know now.   You had a raffle
to raise funds, you are still a little short of sufficient to enable you to rejoin your family in
Philadelphia whence you were lured by the
false promise of work in this great city—you
want a little to buy your return ticket, Eh ?'

"'No, boss,' answered the other with a chuckle,
'that ain't it.'

"My friend who is, in his own opinion, a great
reader of character and the motives of men, was

somewhat nonplussed. 'Ah,' he said, 'I know now. Your baby is dead—you know the little one with the dimples and golden hair that used to crow when she heard your footsteps and lisp 'Papa.' She died in your arm at grey day this morning. There is no fire on the hearth ; no bread on the table ; no money in the house ; the heartless landlord threatens to turn you out ; the form of the one you loved so dearly may be taken by the unfeeling authorities to an unknown grave and you want to raise enough to inter it decently ; for it grieves you sorely to think that the stranger's alien hand may touch the body of the little darling that God has taken and that loved you so, Eh ? '

" 'No, boss,' answered the other, with a rising guffaw, ' that ain't it.'

" Utterly beaten, in a dejected and much injured tone my friend faltered, ' Well, I give up. What *do* you want ? '

" 'Why,' said the other in a surprised way, 'I want to get a darn good hooker of whiskey.'

"And he got it and more too," continued the Stenographer, "and I have brought him here among the worshipers at the shrine of truth. 'Magna est veritas et prevalebit,' and a man who would thus proclaim it when so sorely tempted is one after my own heart and well fit to associate with this goodly company. What say you all ? " An unanimous " Aye " was the response from the others.

. The Coroner seemed to be studying the new comer. As it was that gentleman's custom to look at everybody with a view of seeing how he or she or it would do to "Sit on," his scrutiny passed unnoticed.

The Stenographer continued : "Our friend has promised to give us a discourse or an autobiographical sketch which I believe will be well worth hearing."

The Stranger cooled the poker again and after wiping his mouth with a small and not too clean rag, he began :

I repeat, gentlemen, I am the victim of circumstances. Educated at one of the leading colleges of this country, I have given up what men call prospects. I am by choice a philoso pher, a citizen of the world, or, if you will, a tramp.

I began life as a cook on a trading vessel— a tramp schooner they call it—my intention being to see all I could, and I have seen my share of this terraqueous sphere.

Most of you are men who have settled down to some humdrum pursuit or calling and dare not leave it.

And toil, even pleasant,—continuous toil, day after day in the one eternal groove or routine eats into your daily existence like a chain around a tree, loose and harmless once but the bark of your lives grows over it and to remove it lacerates, hurts and even kills.

You are perhaps hoarding up money for child en who would be better without it. Very probably you have never been a hundred miles from where you sit. Behold in me no Prometheus bound by the Mercury of business to the Mount Caucasus of daily labor.

I assure you, gentlemen, that I have seen almost every prominent city in the world, many towns and nearly every village in the United

States. I know all the customs and some of the traditions of all peoples in all lands. Who of you can say this much? Not one. Your truest student is the traveler. And who so equipped for the road, or in such light marching order as the tramp? His jewelry gives him no trouble; he has none. His luggage requires no special attention; he has none. His servants do not bother him; he has none. He is not the victim of confidence men who desire his money; he has none. Those who do him a kindness do it through motives of charity, not with the expectation of the douceur or tip, hence the kindness is so much more welcome to the beneficiary, for he is known to be poor; for that charity rarest and best is given without money and without price. His mind is not distracted by any of the innumerable cares and troubles that worry and vex the ordinary traveler; his senses of hearing and seeing not rendered less acute; his understanding not dulled; his enjoyment not lessened by the thousand and the one little things that so seriously interfere with the pleasures of travel and sight seeing. He can surely find a place to sleep, a crust to eat, and good water is everywhere free ——

"Pardon me," the Stenographer said, "you promised a sketch of your life, and as you have been at one time a stenographer I am sure the company would be pleased to hear you. The lies—I mean that subject has been under discussion for some time here and doubtless you can throw some further light on it."

After the sizzing made by plunging the hot poker into the beer had subsided, the Stranger resumed :

"Yes, I have among other things followed that profession. I was knocked out by the typewriter.

"When young and innocent I perused with avidity the works of Billings, studied the phonetic style of spelling advocated by Elisha Brandt and others, and read the *Phonetic News*, which Dean Alvord thought was 'Frantic Nuts.' In writing such a word as 'believe,' when doutful whether the 'i' or 'e' came first, I would simply make a 'u' with a dot over the middle of it ; and by such tricks, and using poor handwriting to cover bad spelling, I got along for a while——

"But don't you think, sir," the Stenographer began, "that the present method of spelling is sadly in need of reform? It does seem that fully one-eighth of the letters used in the so-called spelling are of no value, being either silent or misleading, and simply serve to make its pronunciation difficult and its orthography well nigh impossible of attainment. Who would think of writing p-h-l-e-g-m for 'flem' if he were not told, contrary to reason and common sense, that the former was the authorized and orthodox method of spelling?   What a needless waste of alphabetical characters !   If letters are silent what do we want with them in English words ? As much use are they as the bunghole of a barrel after the barrel itself has been destroyed."

"Aha ! " remarked the Stranger, with a shrug, " you put it well, and what you say may be true enough ; yet there are other reforms far more needful in—I cannot bear to say ' English ' language, I prefer to call it ' United States.'   We have our own laws, our own customs and our own form of government. We have our own land, our own flag, and certainly, as a nation, I think we are strong enough to have our own language."

"We use the term English," the other interposed, "merely to show the origin of the words in the language."

"Stop right there," the Stranger said ; "you just quoted the word 'phlegm' as a word to be reformed in spelling, *i. e.*, English spelling. It is not an English word at all, hence your argument is inapplicable ; this being a Greek root the method of spelling it serves to indicate its origin from $\Phi\lambda\acute{\epsilon}\mu\alpha$.

"We know that our Common law is, in a measure, taken from that of England, but the most abject American citizen, if on trial for any offence, cannot be deprived of the right of trial under the laws of the United States.

"We have our flag ; true there may be in it some of the colors of the 'Union Jack,' but nevertheless it is our own Stars and Stripes—our own banner that floats over a free people, its glory as undimmed and its stars as brilliant as when the first thirteen gemmed the azure. It may be taken from the ensign of Great Britain, but it is our banner, and we will uphold it now as we did

"'When Freedom, from her mountain height,
Unfurled her Standard to the air,
And tore the azure robes of night
To set the stars of glory there.'

"No matter what its origin, it is ours, and we will maintain it and sustain it at all hazards.

"As with the flag, so with the language. No

matter whence it came, it is ours ; therefore I
am not speaking English to you but United
States."

"Good ! " cried the Coroner, with animation,
"that's the way to strike it ! "

"Correct sir, quite correct," chimed the Engineer with enthusiasm, while the Real Estate
man ejaculated, "Of course."

"The same is true of our land.   'Twas Eng-

"As with the flag so with the language. No matter whence it
came, it is ours; therefore I am not speaking English to you but
United States."

land's once but is so no longer. We wrested it
from her ; it is ours ; and do you think of calling
this land English? Of course not.

"The same with our customs ; they may have
been adopted or adapted from England, France,
or goodness knows where, but they are ours. As

we have our own flag, our own land, our own customs and our own laws, so we have our own language—that is, the language of the United States.   See?"

"Well," said the Stenographer, thoughtfully, there may be some logic in that ; but to return to the question.   Do you not think it high time to reform the wretched spelling in vogue to-day that violates all rules of euphony, phonetics and common sense ?   What an immensity of time is wasted and what rivers of ink in the writing or printing of so many silent, useless unmeaning letters.   The present spelling is misleading and reform——"

"That will come in good time, sir.   We have not yet reached that point, for there is another and more important matter in relation to our language which demands our attention."

"Well, what can that be ?"

"It is to have a more comprehensive meaning, or rather a more exact definition of words in order that they might convey an exact idea."

"Pshaw !" answered the Scribe, with some asperity, "how can that be so ?   Where is there a language so beautiful, so abounding in words and phrases, that gives with such exactitude the finest shades or distinctions of meaning as the English——"

"There you go again," the Stranger corrected, "United States, please."

"Well, United States," answered the Stenographer testily ; "it is the most subtle, the richest of all spoken tongues to-day in words or phrases which express to the finest point of perfection the idea of the speaker or writer and with absolute mathematical exactitude."

"Bosh!" retorted the Stranger with emphasis.
"Bosh and buncombe. If the purpose of a language is to conceal thought, as it is somewhere
claimed, I grant you the English—excuse me—
United States is most powerful; but I am far
from admitting that such is the purpose of
speech. Now the point I was coming to was
this: many words in our language are extremely inexact, and this is where the reform is
most essential, in my opinion. Take, for instance, the word ' very ;' poor little word! What
a multitude of states and conditions it covers.
A man is very sick. How sick is he? Confined
to his bed? Seriously ill? Dying? 'Very'
tells you nothing. One is 'very' good or 'very'
bad. You perceive that the word gives to
the mind no definite idea of degree at all. It does
not show how much or to what extent the third
person may be sick, or good or bad. Where,
then, the 'absolute mathematical exactitude'
you have referred to? The poor adverb covers
such a vast field that it is utterly unmeaning, for
forty men or forty hundred may be 'very' good
but they are all good to the same extent according to this expression. It is extremely incon-
cise even when used with the adjective. Now,
this defect or lack of meaning in such a word—
the failure to convey the idea—is so appreciated
by the ordinary man that he has adopted a word
now common in the vernacular, which I may
call the superlative degree of the adverb 'very'
—the inelegant but explosive d——"

The Host, who had been nodding, seemed to
suddenly wake up at this remark, and affected
that he had simply been in deep thought, but
with indifferent success.

"I am reminded of this by one of those little incidents not uncommon in a great city. On a recent occasion I observed a crowd gathered in a busy street. Edging my way through it I saw in the centre of the gaping people a street gamin grieviously wounded; his leg had been broken by a runaway horse. The little fellow manfully bore the pain which must have been severe, as it was what surgeons call a compound comminuted fracture. The jagged end of the broken bone projected through the flesh, and I saw at once, from the position of the wound, the color of the blood and the manner in which it flowed, that an artery had been severed and the boy would bleed to death if not attended to at once. I took a handkerchief, knotted it, and having found the break on the blood vessel placed the knot over it and by means of the turniquet stopped the flow, and endeavored to make the lad as comfortable otherwise as possible, till the arrival of the ambulance some time later.

"Perhaps the boy's life was saved by this prompt and heroic treatment, but that is neither here nor there. While engaged in this I was somewhat amused by the expressions of those who crowded about the scene. I think every man said to all the rest: 'Git back there.' 'Give him air.' 'Go for the ambulance.' 'Git a doctor,' &c. Everyone had a suggestion and a remedy; and expressions of sympathy and regret were heard on all sides: 'How shocking!' 'Oh, how sad!' 'So sorry!' &c. A practical man who aided me with the injured boy finally turned to the crowd, saying: 'Good people, you are all sorry for this poor lad, and I am sorry, too. Now,' he said, taking off his hat, into which he dropped a coin, 'What is the extent of our sorrow? I am sorry fifty cents, how much sorry are you?' This proceeding had two good results; it diminished the crowd and brought out a practical response from those who remained."

"Now, the reform I propose," the stranger continued, 'is to give the adverb and adjective a positive and mathematical meaning so as to obviate the use of senseless idiotic expressions that convey no idea of degree, quantity, quality, or condition. Under the new order of things, instead of using the word 'very' bad, or 'too' bad, or 'very' ill, one may say, I am ill. To the natural inquiry, How much so? the response will be, "22 ill" or some such answer. Then you can know just how ill the speaker is, 100 being the extreme degree or normal point beyond which one cannot go or be.

"Then you will hear the remark, 'I am 15 glad, 42 delighted, 64 sad, 24 pleased, 82 astounded, 96 disgusted,' &c., &c.—instead of the wretched 'very' glad, or 'too' sad, or 'much' astounded, or some other such silly, unmeaning phrase. This, you observe, would be a sensible reform. For example, a witness, in giving sworn testimony, who says an event happened quickly, will be asked, "how quickly?" The reply will be, 96 quick, for instance, and the listeners will comprehend just exactly what is meant. Horsemen appreciate to a great extent this vagueness of expression and in their own way have done something to obviate the difficulty. Whoever hears one of them say that a horse went 'very quick-

ly,' or at 'great speed?' The expression in
use by them is that such and such a horse went
a 2.30 or 2.40 gait, or they mention a figure
which has a definite meaning. You have a sum
to rely on and comprehend precisely what is
meant by the speaker. There may be doubt
about the speed, but none about the statement.
'Very' in the instance referred to would indicate a horse going at all gaits from a four-minute
trot to a mile a minute run ; this is due to the
weakness and inefficiency of the expression.
There are many such words that, like charity,
cover a multitude—or rather have to stretch so
far that there is no substance left in them.

"If, or rather *when* we have reformed the language in this wise so that a man speaks and you
know his meaning, your friend may remark :
'Last night I was at the dinner of the Humbug
Club. Before going I was 39 gloomy, but the
company was 83 good, the dinner 99 perfect, the
wine 74 excellent, and after the final toast, I lost
all the gloom, became 23 philosophical, then 63
cheerful and finally reached 98 exhilarated.'
You would understand, of course, just what
manner of men he fell in with. The sinfulness
of his course, the danger he ran would be apparent and hence you could use this most convincing, because mathematical, argument, 'But don't
you know, my dear fellow, that 98 exhilaration
is so much above the normal 12, that you
have exhausted the supply of exhilaration for
nine days, and you cannot have any more till
next week ? You have also overdrawn on philosophical 11, and cheerfulness 42, and you will
have 53 disgust, and 27 remorse for the next

fortnight. Now, does this pay?' This argument which you can cipher on a slate like a sum in proportion, based on exact figures, will be simply unanswerable. All the pulpit orations, all the pamphlets you can print, all the appeals for morality, all the threats of future punishment or disaster, and all the good advice that you can din into your friend's ears about it being 'very' bad for him, &c., will not come home to him like this simple but positive mathematical statement. And he will doubtless govern himself accordingly and endeavor to preserve that daily allowance of the normal amount of contentment, satisfaction, cheerfulness, &c., which is given to every individual in certain mathematical proportions. The person appealed to in this exact way will be vigilant and careful so as not to suffer any dimunition in the normal quantity of the good attributes, and a consequent over draught or influx of remorse, disgust, or unhappiness so far above the normal. This is the first point of reform, speaking——'

"Speaking figuratively," the Lawyer murmured, with just the least tinge of a smile in his voice.

The Stranger winked, almost audibly, and went on :

"Where was I? Oh, at reform spelling. 'To return to our muttons,' as the French say, I endeavored to carry out the idea of reform in spelling, and I subsequently found that the improved method, while most philosophical, was not appreciated by merchants and business men, who preferred the style of spelling in general use, and, while in reality a reformer, I was looked upon as an ignoramus.   Hence, I was often, as boys say, 'on my uppers.'   I became too much disheartened at repeated failures to retain a situation, and, finally, did not try to.

"Ordinarily, if a person is in doubt about the spelling of a word, he writes it, and, looking at it, the eye notes anything peculiar or abnormal in its appearance.   This is not so much the case with the stenographer, who, as a general thing, spells by sound.

"Now, gentlemen, this brings me to the (please put that poker in again) discussion of two of the great senses of the five, in fact, *the* two : hearing and seeing.   Now, the delights of the eye—vision—may be all well enough, but the important sense is hearing.   Smelling, I consider more a sense belonging to, useful to, and only acute in animals.   I dare say it is more a source of pain than pleasure to man.

"Take the blind man,—one utterly deprived of vision, he is generally a self-sustaining person, and always a useful member of society.   Deprived of sight though he is, the other senses become so preternaturally acute as to almost, if not wholly, supply the loss of it.   The sense of touch, as we all know, is really wonderful in the blind.   But whoever heard of the sense of touch so sharply developed in the deaf man ?   Surely he would seem to require it in all its preternatural acuteness, as much as his sightless brother. A blind person, though deprived of the sense of physical vision, as I may call it, still has the keenest "insight" or appreciation of the fine arts of poetry and music, which not only soothe the savage breast, but lift mere men to the portals of heaven.

"Your deaf man, on the contrary, is generally a dullard. If his other senses be abnormally acute he has no way of indicating it, and suffers under his misfortune till the welcome end. Being deaf, he is generally dumb—dumb, because he does not hear sounds, and hence cannot make them, for man is an imitative animal, and therein does Darwin find the 'missing link' between man and the monkey—mainly in the imitative faculty of the latter.

"I have simply stated this, gentlemen, to show you the great importance of sounds and sound-writing, *i. e.*, phonography.

"Natural sounds are to-day as they were in the beginning, and doubtless will be when the arch-angel's trumpet bids the dead arise and come to judgment. It has been well-said that the lark now carols the same song and in the same key as when Adam first turned his enraptured ear to catch the moral. The owl first hooted on B-flat, and it still loves the key. The three chirps of the cricket have been in B since Tubal Cain first heard them in his smithy, or the Israelites in their ash-ovens. Never has the buzz of the gnat risen above the second A, nor that of the house fly's wing sunk below the first F."

The Host here broke in :

"But don't you think, sir, that the voice of the Jersey mosquito is deeper, broader in tone, denser, more earnest, business-like and sleep-banishing now, than it was some ages ago, owing to that animal's wonderful physical progress and mental development, arising from the constant imbibition or transmission of the fine blood ____"

Disdaining to notice this unseemly interruption, the other continued :

"The breaking of the storm-billows on the beach is still the same mighty roar as it was in the beginning, when 'the Spirit of God moved over the waters.'   The wind still shrieks through the rigging of our sailing vessels as it did through the cordage of 'the two ships that stood by the lake at Gennesareth.'   The murmur of the brook and the gurgling sound of flowing water is the same to day as it was when the elder servant of the house of Abraham drank from the pitcher of Rebecca, and this applies to other fluids besides water, gentlemen.

"Listen ! "

The Stranger here raised the pitcher high over the empty glass, which he filled to the brim, and resumed :

" I have even attempted to describe sounds in verse, which, after I take this, I will give you. You hear the hiss of the poker in this beaker. To me the sound is not unpleasant, but if I were to hear either of you gentlemen attempting to make a similar sound with your organs of speech, while I am speaking, I should be much offended."

After three or four repetitions of a noise like that made by extracting a rubber shoe out of soft mud, the Stranger wiped his mouth on the rag, cleared his throat, and, with considerable dramatic effect, recited what he called

SOUNDS.

I.

What cheer in the shout of the mast-head lookout
  To the exile returning home,
Who, tired of war, in countries afar,
  Is crossing the salt sea foam?
The expectant eye would land descry
  Beneath the shading hand,
When loud and clear breaks on his ear
  The welcome cry of " Land ! "

II.

How sweet to rest on Earth's green breast
  On a balmy summer's day,
And hear the bleat of the browsing sheep,
  Or the rustle of new-mown hay ;
But sad to hear the sob so drear
  Over the still, white dead,
And the hollow tones of clay and stones
  As they fall on the coffin lid.

III.

How soft, how sweet, is the "tweet, tweet, tweet,"
  Of the mating birds, in spring,

And what so gay as children's play,
　When their laugh makes the welkin ring?
In clear moonlight, on a frosty night,
　How fierce the bark of "Tray,"
When the faithful brute hears the stealthy foot
　As it treads its devious way.
Not loud, but worse, comes the muttered curse
　From the felon's close-set jaw,
Within the grasp, the iron clasp,
　And sudden clutch of the law.

IV.

Soft and low, in the bright fire's glow,
　Is the old cat's pleasant purr,
From his place so snug on the cosy rug,
　At each stroke of the silky fur ;
But sharp the yowls and fierce the howls
　Made by the same old cat,
When the sleepless and rash, at the window sash,
　In the upper room of the flat,
Sneak vengefully back for the big boot-jack
　To throw it out like a shot :
While the nimble puss, with a m-e-a-o-w and a
　　whiz,
　Laughs in a sheltered spot.

V.

What seemeth only to the watcher lonely
　At the dying couch of the sick,
To measure the gloom in the silent room
　Like the clock's monotonous tick,
So steady and slow, as hither and fro
　It ticks, then ticks again ;
But like whisper of hell is the shriek of the shell
　As it bursts amid sleeping men.

VI.

As the coo of the dove is the murmur of love,
　When youth is free and fair,
And the future seems all pleasant dreams,
　With naught of trouble or care.

Sweet whisper of bliss in love's first kiss,
  But time turns the wheel—and pshaw !
How glibly flung from the supple tongue
  Is the taunt of the mother-in-law.

VII.

What so loud as the thunder-cloud
  That breaks on the listening ear ?
What so fine as the low of the kine
  When homing time grows near ?
The purling brook in·a pebbly nook
  Hath the softest murmur of all ;
And a dread, quaint sound seems to resound
  In the " ping " of the minie ball.

VIII.

How slow to the weary is the time ; how dreary,
  How welcome the six o'clock bell,
Bidding workers depart who've acted their part
  To rest for another brief spell ;
At its loud, joyous clamor, the wheel and the
    hammer,
  May wait until called on again ;
But what echo's so shrill o'er valley and hill
  As the toot of the " wild-cat " train.

———

All nature abounds with the quaintest of sounds
  And what so appalling, yet mild,
When silent and dark, the night waneth—hark !
  'Tis the moan of a dying child !

The ominous silence which settled on the
company was broken by the Stenographer, who
muttered something about all this being very
fine but hardly relevant to the subject under
discussion.

" I am coming to that," the other said—" in
fact I am right at it now. The subject of short
hand is one which, though interesting to a great

number of people, there is a great deal of humbug about.   The art is looked at generally as if
it were something entirely new and simple.   The
fact is, the easier it may be as a study the slower
it is in practice.   It is not enough to comprehend and retain its principles ; they must be put
in practice, systematically and perseveringly, or
not at all.

"And to its being a modern thing I will only
quote one of the oldest and best adepts of the
art in the country, who, in his time, was called
by the late William Smith O'Brien the 'recording angel.'   I quote from memory, gentlemen,
because my library is not accessible just now.
Ahem !

"'Systems of writing designed to keep pace
with speech have at all times enjoyed the privilege of awakening the curiosity of young persons
disposed to study, and of attracting the attention of people devoted to intellectual pursuits.
What higher satisfaction could, in fact, be offered
to the man of learning or of letters than that
which would supply the implements whose use
would enable him to secure instantaneously
whatever might strike him in a discourse, an im-
provisation, or a dramatic representation ; a
means which would empower the poet, the dra-
matist or the novelist to fix, at will, the inspira-
tions, often glowing but always fleeting, that at
times light up his imagination, and which he re-
grets his inability to retain in his memory with
all their first vivid coloring?   To fasten his
thoughts as rapidly as they present themselves
would establish his mastery over them and aug-
ment the activity of his imagination.   Therefore

one can readily understand why the creation of
an instrument so valuable should have engaged
the attention of learned men of lofty merit, such
as Leibnitz, Porta, Condorcet, &c., who were
sustained, perhaps, by the hope of restoring an
art once so flourishing as we can readily conjec-
ture by an inspection of the system of Tyro and
the semiography of the ancients.   For, long before the time of the Knickerbockers ; long before
America was dreamed of, except in old Irish
prophecies ; long before Charlemagne sat on the
throne of Western Europe ; long before the Sar-
acens had invaded Spain or the Saxons had set
foot in Britain ; long before the Roman cut-
throats who fled into the Pontine marshes had
carried off the Sabine women—the grand old
philosophical Greeks had, according to Dion
Cassius, their ' half letters ' or short hand "——

The cynical Host here broke in : "And long
before Billy Patterson was struck by the man
in the iron mask, and long before Junius wrote
the Mulligan letters"——

The Stenographer, with a warning wave of the
hand and a muttered " sh," cut short the interruption.

The Victim of Circumstances resumed : " As
I have said, there is more humbug to the square
inch in stenography than in anything else, not
excepting the occult sciences—theosophy, mind-
reading, palmistry, cryptomancy, professional
jugglery, the new sciences of painting sounds or
weighing thoughts, etc.   One-quarter tuition or
twelve easy lessons, and you have it.

" Seduced, like others, by brilliant promises, I
studied one of the methods in vogue, and, by

means of it, attained skill enough to write **three** or four times more rapidly than by the ordinary method ; but when I tried to follow a speaker, even the most deliberate, or a dramatic declamation, I made a complete failure of it. Having had occasion afterwards to impart my painful confidence to persons who had studied the abbreviative art, in methods different from those I had followed, they acknowledged that my experience had been almost their own. At the same time the superior and well-established capacity of those persons not permitting me to attribute their lack of success to the cause which I assumed led to my own failure I was naturally encouraged, and believed that non-success was due to the inefficiency of the means rather than the inaptitude of the scholar.

"It all comes down to what our greatest poet, Longfellow, says :

     ' Art is long and time is fleeting.'

"(Yes, if you will, please fill it again.) To show that you are really and truly gazing on the victim of circumstances I shall relate one instance which this subject brings up that occurred in my little life.

CHAPTER XXVIII.

THE STRANGER'S STRANGE NARRATIVES.

"I DID a gigantic corporation a good turn once that is now forgotten, but I shall remember it to my dying day. I was marked as an exhibit in that case and will bear the mark to my grave. I prevented a robbery by the exercise of my art——"

" *You* did," said the Engineer increduously. "Aye," said the other, "I saved the pay-car." "Oh," added the Engineer, "what we call the Salvation car?"

"Yes," returned the Stranger, "I was the humble means of preventing a well planned robbery."

"And, of course," said the Host, "you got the presidency for it?"

"No, indeed," answered the Stranger, sadly. "I got jugged, assaulted, and nearly sent up to do time for the State."

"For saving a train?" the Engineer inquired, wonderingly.

"Certainly," rejoined the Stranger. "To relieve your anxiety I will narrate it with as few words as possible:

"Years ago, when I became a traveler on the road, I had tramped and trucked a few hundred miles from San Francisco, and I may say in passing you never experience the real exhilaration of railroad travel until you 'truck' it at 50 miles an hour or so. You are fixed in one position, without daring to change, the ground flying under you, death within a few inches of your nose all the time, your feet and hands extended and braced against the iron work of the truck unable to make the slightest move-ment. The least slip means destruction. Below the car the dust is often so thick that you can cut it with a shovel and the awful smell of hot oil and steam which is the peculiarity of rapidly moving trains is almost stifling. It is danger-ously exhilarating and no mistake.

I had gone several hundred miles as I say in this manner and was disturbed by an oiler as we stopped at a way-station. I hardly know where it was—several miles from Syrroltown, wherever that is. I didn't care much, but I wanted to reach New York. I remember asking a smart young man at the freight house what state I was in, and on his answering that I was in a state of dilapi-dation I left him and trudged on over the ties. I footed it for quite a distance, and—pardon this further digression, but I take this occasion to remark that constructors of American railroads have, as I firmly believe, intentionally placed the ties in such a position as to tire out the most energetic pedestrian who undertakes to walk on the wood work over the road-bed. The ties are too close for ordinary stepping and to skip one so as to walk on each alternate tie makes the steps so long that fatigue soon supervenes. It has always seemed to me that this was the in-tention of the companies—the ties are placed as they are with malice aforethought because the more distressing walking becomes the more anxious people are to ride. See?

The Real Estate Man nodded : " Quite so."

I trudged on, as I say, until I had gone many miles. Judging from the speech and dress of the few people I met, the deep cuts in the road and slaty condition of the banks, I believe I was somewhere in Northern Ohio. I soon became tired, and at a desolate-looking way-station I noticed an empty cattle car side-tracked, and getting on the "off-side" of it found the lattice door open. Quickly entering it I made myself at home, as much so as if I had chartered the car, which I really had done, except that I had not paid for it.

In the upper end of the car there was a quantity of hay and as the weather was tolerably mild I made myself comfortable in it and took a long and much needed nap. How long I slept, I knew not. I was awakened by the bump of the car and the clank of the coupling pin that told me my car was hooked on and was soon whirling over the ground at a good lively pace, nearly forty miles an hour as I judged. I can generally tell the speed of a train by one of two simple calculations; counting the telegraph poles, or observing the frequency with which the wheels strike the ends or joints of the thirty foot rails; that is, so many feet in a second. For want of a watch I have my pulse with me, and if that fails me (it is seldom out of tune) I can tell within a fraction of the length of a minute by repeating Hamlet's soliloquy or a certain number of lines of Paradise Lost; ergo: so many feet to a rail, so many rails to a minute or to a mile. For instance, five thirty feet rails to every two seconds, or a hundred and fifty feet is a fraction over fifty miles an hour. If I hear the jolt of the wheels on the rail-joint twice every second, that is sixty feet or forty miles an hour about."

The speaker paused and glanced furtively at the Engineer as the latter passed his hand wearily over his forehead and shut his teeth hard on a fresh cud.

I hoped to reach some civilized community before nightfall. As I lay among the hay I began to be racked by a most intolerable thirst, which was somewhat aggravated by the strong, dry odor of the hay with which I was covered.

My thirst increased to such a degree that I was about to indicate my presence to the brakeman on the forward car and take my chance of getting "fired," when I felt the train slowing up. Approaching the wicket-door and looking out I observed that it was dusk.

Before the engine had fully stopped on the east side of the "Y" I dropped lightly to the ground and ran along to the station. Finding water in the freight house I took a good pull, and having procured a sandwich returned to my car, which I re-entered on the safe side—opposite the station. I had hardly re-entered, when looking out I saw the disconnected engine and forward cars cross the "Y" to the main track, leaving the cattle car, in which I was, to my great disgust, at a standstill. As I glanced at the moving train the rear brakeman seemed to be making a motion either to me or to the station agent, and I heard him shouting something which I did not catch.

Fearing discovery and desiring to retain my comfortable quarters, I looked about the car for a better hiding place than the loose hay. I then observed what I had not before noticed, two empty ale casks in a corner of the car, one head-

less and - both bungless. The first of these I
raised, turned the headless end down and tipped
it over my head. Crouching on the floor on
which the chimes rested the barrel effectually
concealed me. Once in it I turned in such a
way that my eyes and ears were in close proximity to the open bunghole. Here I made myself
as comfortable as the cramped quarters would
permit and waited. Nor had I long to wait. I
soon heard the station master stumbling about
the car, and peering through the aperture I saw
him swing his lantern around and heard the
rustle of the dry hay under his heavy feet.
Coming to the other end of the car where I was
he kicked the barrel which enveloped me with a
muttered : "Darn the tramp, I'll fix him ; I guess
he is in the other."

The man left the car, and I kept extremely
quiet for fully half an hour. I was about to
change from my restricted and uncomfortable
position, when hearing the rumble and noise of
a moving engine, I concluded to keep just where
I was till we were fairly coupled and on the
road. In a few moments I felt the bumper
strike the draw-head, which always makes a peculiar sound, as you know, sir, unless as too
often happens some poor fellow's body serves as
a cushion, to prevent injury to the coupling gear
of the car.

The engine had hardly taken up the slack,
and I was just about to tilt my house over and
emerge, when I heard a suppressed voice saying: "Jump in boys ; easy, now." By the noise
of the shuffling feet I judged I had at least half
a dozen others for company. "Whistle for

Jack," said the same voice, and I put my ear to the bunghole.

I have a musical ear, gentlemen, and if the new comers were philosophers of the road I would know the signal. It is the tuning gamut of the banjo on the open strings, beginning with A on the second space, and ending with the three G's below the second ledger line. Had this been the signal I should have kicked over my barrel and welcomed the new comers with that fellow feeling which makes us wondrous kind. I heard the whistle. It was a railroad signal, a long toot and three short ones, and I thought it better to wait a while before pro· claiming my presence.

The man called Jack reached the car before it had got under headway, and I could hear that he was being assisted to enter. The group came up to the corner where I was, and I began to feel somewhat uneasy. One of the men sat on the head of the barrel which enclosed me, and I could feel and appreciate the noise his heels made as he swung them against the staves of the cask.

By the time we had settled into a steady run I heard one of the parties say : " Now, do you fellows all understand it ? " " I do," one remarked.

" Well, I ain't got it down very fine," another answered. " That's funny, too," the first voice continued. " The pay train comes in at the Saloonville station ; that is 50 miles from any-wheres. No one near there but the telegraph operator, and the side track is most three miles from it. Tom, Jack and you get be-

hind the trees, and you fellows are tamping
on the road and jump on as she slows up.
Bill gets in the caboose, as he knows the
engineer, and gets up a game—euchre, or
anything that will bring the crew to the front;
he goes back and pulls the pin as the engine
crosses the switch so as to sidetrack the pay-
train.   It's easy enough—just the same as
making a flying switch, and she will be going
slow over that bit of road ; anyhow‚ you must
be right there to throw the switch when Bill
waves his hand that the pin is out. You wait
till 95 gets on the main and you throw it to cut
off the 'pay,' see? It is the only car on. To
do it you've got to be spry."

"I should think he would," the Engineer put
in with just a faint tone of doubt. "To throw
a switch between the wheels of two trucks when
a train is moving, even slowly, requires some
agility. But excuse me. Go right on."

"I am simply telling you what I heard," the
Stranger resumed. "Another of the fellows
then remarked, "Is it the 'pay' sure ?"

"Yes," said the one I took to be the leader.

"Do you think," another spoke up, "They
will leave it unprotected like that?"

"There will be only one man on it at most,"
the first speaker returned, "because they don't
suspect anything here. If he is ugly we will
make short work——"

"Well, I didn't come to do any of that kind
of business. I know the Company didn't treat
us fair in that strike and put on outsiders. But
I don't go for smashing——"

"No more do we," another says, "but 46 will

stand by us, and if we can do it and get off it'll be no mor'n squaring things and what's the harm? We can prove we weren't there if anything does happen. Bill says he can show an aliby."

At this there was a general laugh and I began to be a little startled. Here were men with a real or pretended grievance against a corporation. They had evidently conspired systematically to rob the pay train on the road. As I gathered some were to make a pretence of repairing the road; one of them was to engage the attention of the operator at the point near the proposed looting; another acquainted with the engineer was to board and coax the trains' crew to the caboose and disconnect the pay car which as I understood was at the rear of the train; a third was to throw the switch, in order to side track it and the gang were to plunder it at their leisure. I confess I was somewhat startled.

Between the heat of my close quarters and my fear of discovery I felt the cold sweat running down my face. I held my breath and no living man can tell the awful tortures I suffered in my wretched cramped position. It was then too late for me to acknowledge my preser.ce. These fellows would know that I had heard the programme discussed, and in order to carry out their designs they might make short work of me. I must remain quiet at all hazards. I think I would have given ten years of my life for an opportunity to sneeze, but I suppressed the terrible temptation by the most heroic effort. I felt that under-the circumstances it might cost me dearly, and my position was not one to be sneezed at.

Hunger and thirst I have grappled with but they are nothing in comparison to what one suffers when endeavoring to choke off or postpone a sneeze or cough, which if allowed to escape would imperil one's life.

How I passed the night in that place you can hardly imagine. I stood it somehow, and soon knew by the freshness of the air that daylight was breaking. I gathered from the chat of my companions that we had scarce fifty miles to go, a journey of less than two hours as we were then traveling.

After a while we began to slow up and I heard my fellow passengers making prepara tions to leave. Our car was to continue on, though we were to wait a short time on the switch to let the 8.30 pass us.

As we slowed up they all left the car and the other train passed us at a rapid rate. I waited till my fellow travelers were some distance away before emerging from my hiding place. I had no burning desire to let them know that their plans had been heard. There was a curve in the road near by and when they reached it and turned, I felt that I might leave unobserved; at that point I dropped off and started to walk slowly behind the others who were some few hundred yards away. Shortly after the train started to reach the next switching point some eighteen miles distant. It was scarcely out of sight before I bitterly regretted my want of thought in not acquainting the train hands with what I had heard.

Here I was in a desolate part of the line, no one near but half a dozen desperate men bent on committing a crime, and single-handed I could not hope to cope with them.

True, in an isolated freight shanty some miles up the road there was a telegraph operator. He was in all probability alone, and would soon be in the clutches of these lawless fellows; moreover there was no train due on this line till several hours after the pay car train.

I thought of all this and cursed myself for my stupidity in letting the train go, without an effort on my part to state the condition of affairs to the company's employees.

When I looked at the situation of things, I tried to convince myself that it was not my business to interfere. Perhaps it was all for the best, and if the railroad company could stand it, why not I? In all probability these men had been ill-treated, and were actuated solely by what is called the wild justice of revenge. I soon dismissed this sophistry as I thought of the many poor wives so anxiously awaiting the arrival of the pay-car, and finally concluded it was my bounden duty as a man to do my best to prevent the consummation of the crime.

I left the road-bed, struck through a path in the woods, and as I walked along I became so exasperated at my stupidity that I finally sat down under a tree to think it out. Having turned the matter over in my mind, I arrived at the conclusion that there was a bare chance if I hurried on of reaching the operator's hut before the others, in time to warn him, so that he could telegraph for help.

Starting to my feet, I struck out on a good brisk walk through the woods, keeping the telegraph poles in sight for "bearings," in the direction, as I supposed, of the telegraph station.

After a steady half-hour's tramp, in which I lost ground travelling through the woods, I observed smoke arising from the direction of the track, and, conjecturing that it came from the operator's hut, I made for that point.

As I reached the clearing, I saw a rough looking customer just entering the operator's shanty. Quickening my pace, I crossed the threshold before he had hardly time to speak to the operator.

The fellow had the grimy look of a railroad employe, and seemed somewhat displeased at my presence; and, though he addressed me as mate, his manner seemed to indicate that my company was not entirely welcome.

In answer to his interrogatories, I informed him that I was going westward, a fib, on my part, to which he replied : "There ain't nothing here, mate, but, if you go two miles below, there's a farm-house and very nice people, too—never turned a hungry man away. Push right on, mate."

As I had just come from that direction and had seen no farm-house, I felt that my little falsification was quite dwarfed in comparison with his big whopper, but I mentally called it even. I noticed that he, looked rather displeased because I did not leave instantly.

I sauntered over to the operator, whom I thought much too young and effeminate looking for an isolated, lonely-looking spot like that, and was about to whisper to him, when the fellow at the door and another, whom he called Jake, that

I had not previously seen, approached me before I had time to wink, and in a manner that I thought exceedingly threatening.

"Get out, you! Clear! Come, git! Make yourself scarce," the new comer said, authoritatively.

Under the circumstances, I felt that to blurt out my suspicions, or to attempt any conversation with the operator, might lead to my maltreatment by these two burly ruffians. I was no match for either one of them. I endeavored to temporize, but saw at once that they did not intend to give me an opportunity to speak to the telegraph agent, and I concluded it would be foolhardy in the extreme for me to insist upon doing so, at the risk of what might be serious consequences to myself.

In an humble and conciliatory tone, I said: "Well, gents, I am a poor, tired tramp. I just want to rest here a couple of minutes and then I am off."

"Well, make it short and hook it quick," growled Jake's companion.

I looked furtively at the operator, but his glance at me was one of blank, innocent ignorance, and that was all.

I stood gazing out of the window, thinking what was best to be done, and raised my coat sleeve, in a casual way, to wipe off the condensed steam which had formed on the window glass. It came from the kettle on the stove, which was steaming merrily over the little fire, the smoke of which had attracted my attention when the operator was preparing his frugal lunch.

One glance at the window-pane and I adopted a ruse.

"Is that an eagle?" I suddenly cried, looking out of the upper sash.

"Where?" cried Jake and his companion, simultaneously.

"There he goes," I said, "away behind those trees."

They both rushed to the doorway and looked out.

I winked at the operator, and, with my forefinger, made this mark on the window-pane: (Can you read this?) A knowing glance from the young man, as, with a swish of his foot on the saw-dust floor, he answered: (Yes.)

I then, in an apparently absent-minded way, drew, with my fingers, these characters on the steamed and not over-clean glass: —

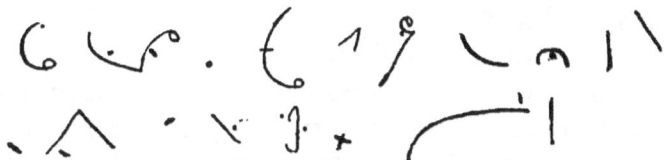

(Good: These fellows, and others on the switch, have made it up to rob the pay-train. Look out!), and moved towards the door to get a better view, as it were, of the "invisible" eagle. In passing, I looked at the floor, near the operator's chair, and saw where his heel had scraped the saw-dust from the floor, leaving a vacant spot, like this: (All right!)

Having observed this and failing, of course, to see the "eagle," I was about returning to my place at the window when Jake's companion interposed his burly form at the threshold, as he growled: "You better go, now. You ain't wanted. Is he?` "Naw," remarked the other, "chuck him."

Without awaiting for anything in the way of physical force that I saw ready for me I left and started to walk down the road. Having gone about a hundred yards I turned abruptly into the woods, approached the hut again at the rear side and put my ear close to the weather boards.

Doubtless Jake and his companion congratulated themselves that the telegraph operator was completely in the dark, and surmised that ever if we did suspect anything and intended to interfere with their plan, we would hardly do so as we were short handed. We were even more short handed than they supposed we were."

The Host here ostentatiously opened the window and gasped.

The Stranger smiled broadly, and resumed : "I saw Jake's companion leave the shanty and walk down towards the switch where his mates were, leaving Jake to divert the attention of the young operator.

Soon the whistle of the pay train was heard, the operator rushed out to give the necessary signal and the "O K" and went in again, while Jake stood in the doorway. The latter then started, as I supposed, down to where he thought the train was to be halted, on a run. I immediately left my place of concealment and went in to chat with the young man, and congratulate myself on having played such a shrewd game on the would-be robbers.

I introduced myself to the operator, and while talking with him about my connection with the

matter, I fancied I heard a whistle.   Being absorbed in my narrative, I gave little attention to
it, supposing that my late traveling companions
were signalling to each other while pursuing the
train on foot, which was doubtless, as the operator said, far out of danger by this time.   I was
detailing with some satisfaction to the operator
how I discovered the plot in all its bearings when
the whistle was repeated close at hand.

A loud shout broke on my ear.

It was near by.

I started to the door with an intuitive perception that my personal safety was in danger.

Too late.

Jake in leaving the hut had made a detour
through the woods as I had, and had observed
me listening at the shanty eaves.   Perhaps he
suspected something of the kind and whistled
softly to his companion.   While waiting for him
he had crouched behind the house after I had
re-entered it, and had heard me narrate my
share in the up-setting of the proposed plan.   In
a short time his companion returned in answer
to his repeated signal, and before I could rush
out they were upon us.

We were no match for them at all.

With oaths and imprecations Jake was at me.
I made a feeble show of fight, but after the first
smash between the eyes I just remember falling
and seeing the rest of the baffled conspirators
rush in to aid Jake and his friend in finishing us
up.

I remember as I was going down seeing Jake's
companion jumping with both feet on the pros-
trate body of the delicate young operator, while
the others took a hand in at me.

After the first two or three heavy kicks I was unconscious, and could never tell for how many hours.

When I came to I was in the lock-up in the nearest village, many miles from the scene of the assault.

I had been almost killed and was dreadfully weak. In fact, nothing saved my life, as I believe, but the crowd about me during the attack, who stood so close to one another that they interfered with each other in their desperate and well-nigh successful attempt to do for me.

As I say, I was in the village jail. Generally prepared as I am for anything that comes along, I was somewhat surprised to find myself in such a place. How I came there is the singular part of this story.

When I recovered sufficiently to know or care about anything, I managed by dint of questioning the old fellow that ran the guard house to discover why I was there.

I really thought that I had suffered enough for justice's sake, and that the villagers, or at least the railroad company, whose property I had almost died in saving, would at least see that a clean bed was provided for me on which to lie——

The Host in a loud whisper suggested: "But, you know, sir, some people don't need it; they can do it anyway——"

The dangerous glitter in the Coroner's gray eye choked off the ironical gentleman.

"And decent food to eat," the stranger continued.

"Well, now, don't you know what you air

here for?" said the farmer jailer to me. "You're a cute one, you air. I guess you'll go up for this."

Subsequently he brought me the village paper saying, "If you can read, this will tell you just what you air here for."

I read it and gasped. "For God's sake, does this refer to me—this account?"

"Why in course," the jailer said with a chuckle. "You're a cooler, you air." I never was so shocked.

The village weekly contained this account of my heroism—I do not think that word is too strong:

DESPERATE ATTEMPT TO ROB A TRAIN.

"On Wednesday last, several blood-thirsty villains, members of the Jones gang of cut-throats, made a determined and well-nigh successful attempt to loot the pay-car on Mug Junction, near Selineville, which passed at 12.30. But for the wise precautions which the officials of the railroad had taken, as per our repeated warnings, the monthly compensation of many of our esteemed townsmen would have been seized by a gang of blood-thirsty and unhung villains. It seems that an endeavor was made to derail the train, which was frustrated by the gallant and vigilant train hands, under the directions of the polite officials of the road, who read and profit by the sound advice given in the columns of the *Horn Blower*. Owing to this, the desperate attempt was unsuccessful, and the pay-car passed on its way unretarded, bringing joy to thousands of happy homes.

"Maddened by their failure, the scoundrels made a concerted attack on the operator at the shanty nearest the scene of the attempted outrage, and, though he defended himself bravely, putting at least one of his assailants *hors du combat*, we hear that young Carson is frightfully if not fatally injured. He was brought to the hospital at the county-seat, and we learned from Mrs. Mulligan, who brought eggs there yesterday morning, that he is not expected to recover. He defended himself with such bravery that one of the scoundrels was left weltering in his gore, and this unhung malefactor is now in the lockup.

"Unfortunately, the other villains escaped, but we shall

deem it our public duty to hunt the rascals down. The cut-throat who is now confined in the lockup, is seriously injured.   Should he recover sufficiently, he will be taken to the county-seat to receive the punishment he so richly deserves.   We regret to state, by later advices, that young Carson is still unconscious, as we learn from that distinguished disciple of Esculapius, the world-famed Dr. Bollus, a constant reader of the *Horn Blower*, who gives little hope of his recovery.

"There are several applicants for young Carson's position but we have not as yet decided whom to support.

"Now is the time to subscribe for the *Horn Blower*. Potatoes and butter taken in subscription.   That this dastardly outrage was nipped in the bud, is due to the persistent warnings published in the brilliant columns of this live paper, is admitted on all sides.   Now is the time to subscribe!   Positively, baled-hay will not be accepted at the desk for subscriptions, under any circumstances."

You smile at this, gentlemen, but I assure you it frightened me. What would be my position, I thought, if the operator, Carson, they called him, should not recover sufficiently to state the facts in the case, or should ignore my part in the transaction altogether as this wretched editor seemed to assume.

I was in a fix and a bad one. This was a farming community, hard-headed, matter-of-fact people. What credence would they give to my story? It seemed to me from the tone of the newspaper and the crowd of open-mouthed villagers that came to stare at me that instead of being looked upon as a peaceful honest man who had gone out of his way and even suffered to prevent a felony, I was in reality considered and exhibited as a most dastardly villain.

The more I thought of the situation the less I liked it, and began to wish that I hadn't been quite so free to offer myself as a martyr in the cause of justice.

If the operator did not come forward who

would believe me? Who would substantiate my statement? Certainly not those who assaulted me. No one saw it besides myself, those who took part in it as my assailants and Carson; and, if he were not capable and willing to help me out of this uncomfortable dilemma, how could I prove that I was not one of the gang? A stranger in a strange land, without friends, alone, I began to curse myself for being a reckless and a meddlesome fool. True, I could deny that I was guilty of a felony, yet, denial is one thing, proof another.

I sincerely hoped for my own sake as well as for his, that Carson would be sufficiently recovered to attend my trial. He failed to appear. I learned afterwards that he had been conscious at one time of his illness during which he had made a partial statement. The company had a dispatch to corroborate this. On the strength of that information the pay car was given the right of way. The operator had failed to state where he derived his information before he again lost consciousness, and he seemed to have forgotten my part of the transaction altogether. In every aspect the outlook for me was exceedingly blue.

I have been in many scrapes and I could perceive that in this one I had struck the worst of them all, and all for no benefit to myself. It was dreadful, but I still hoped that my usual good fortune would stand by me. It was a forlorn hope. The very fact that I had so often and anxiously inquired about the condition of Carson was taken against me. The wise men of the village supposed that my anxiety arose from the fear that I would be charged with his murder if he died.

I declare to you, gentlemen, I was in a hazardous position. The awful beating I had received, the pain of which still racked my body, was nothing to the mental suffering I underwent during those dreary days while waiting to be brought up as a criminal to the County Court.

But I will hurry through and tell you the upshot of it all.

My so-called trial or examination came on. I was indicted for an attempt at grand larceny in the 1st degree and felonious assault, by an idiotic lot of lunkheads called the Grand Jury and the State made what appeared to be a clear case against me.

I was a despised tramp, hence, an incorrigible thief. Friendless, moneyless, powerless, weak and disheartened as I was I attempted to make a true statement of the facts, as I have related them here, to the county judge, one Nore by name, an irascible, fussy old gentleman, perhaps an honest man but I'll never believe it. He refused to even hear me then, and remanded me in the custody of the sheriff. While being conveyed to the jail I endeavored to make a friend of this official and told him my story substantially as I have been telling it to you and offered to depose solemnly to its truth. He listened, rubbing his chin thoughtfully and said with a good deal of native sarcasm when I got through, "Young feller, do you expect anybody around here to swallow that ere yarn? Do you think you can impose on this ere court of ourn by any such stuff as that? She aint to be trifled with I can tell you. Better own up. You'll see you air committed to await the result of this ere murderous assault you have committed on this ere young man." He cut short my protests of innocence as we reached the jail and placed me in the custody of one of his minions with the remark, " Handcuff this villain, officer, and lock him up."

I was finally brought up to plead, my story repeated to the court, and the judge assigned a very young lawyer to defend me ; then I felt that my case was hopeless.

In the dissecting room a " stiff" is sometimes given over to a young surgeon to practice on, and however much he cuts it there is no harm done. I was the first victim this young lawyer had, and whether I was guilty or not made no particular difference; he was going to have the pleasure of talking to the court, he would have his name in the county paper and get some notoriety out of it in any event. But I am rambling too much. I can hardly bear even now to relate coolly that whole wretched business. A great philosopher truly remarks that when a man begins to go down hill everything seems to be greased for the occasion. It was so in my case. Without being too prolix, the upshot of my trial was that I was acquitted in a way, partly because of the friendly interference of a lawyer who represented a rival railroad, and mainly because young Carson recovered. Carson failed to identify me as one of his assailants, but acted as I thought, in a weak, half-hearted way; and, as I verily believe, did his level best to keep all the glory of the thing to himself.

Owing to his failure to identify me and the efforts of the lawyer in the employ of the other company, I was finally acquitted in a way, as I remarked, a sort of a Scotch verdict, "Not proven," was rendered in my case. My counsel insisted on producing the sash on which I said I had written in warning to the operator. It was brought to court, but the steam had long since dried on it, although by holding it to the light some faint traces of dust from the ends of my fingers appeared in odd streaks. The magistrate leaned back and smiled, and of course the jury seeing the judge smile, guffawed at the whole thing as too silly to be considered; however, the statement of the operator that he could not recognize me as one of his assailants, and the fact that the attempt at the looting had been a failure, did more for me than justice (who is always represented blind and is often deaf and dumb) could have done.

I was thrown out of jail, sick, sore and characterless, and got thirty days to leave the county. I told them I didn't need half the time. Thirty minutes would do me. I shook its dust from my wearied feet, and when I got far enough away indulged in good, strong, satisfactory denunciation of the ignorant dogberry and fatheaded jury who would have made a felon out of a martyr, and left the cursed place.

I need scarcely say that this sickened me considerably on the short hand business. Perhaps decency demands that I should add this: Subsequently when young Carson had fully recovered, he was profuse in his apologies, and sent me a family pass to ride free on that railroad.

I have no family ; if I were a Mormon, and "sealed unto" Mrs. Brigham Young and her progeny, I should take good care to keep them a great distance from the Mud Chunk and Selineville Railroad Co.'s roadbed in the State of———

_ That is all. I may say further, in justice to Carson, that he was the means of getting me a position with a certain gentleman, who made me his private secretary.

This was a retired lav_er and a great bookworm, who lived at his country seat, not far from Trenton. Here I had free access to his large library, and many of the creature comforts which, to ordinary men, make up the pleasures of life, although there was a routine sameness about it not entirely to my liking. My employer had a ward, his niece, who was on a visit to Mr. Mason, near Philadelphia, an old friend of her guardian. The lawyer's daughter had conceived an aversion to the ward, which, I think, was one of the reasons for the latter's protracted visit at Mason's. This daughter made it a constant practice to open all letters which came to her father. I cannot tell you how much this annoyed me, or why it should do so. I was not fool enough to complain of it to him. I assumed he knew it, and believe it vexed him quite as much as it disgusted me. Somewhat under the influence of the daughter, as I thought, he did not seem anxious to assert his rights in this respect, and it was not for me to interfere.

On one occasion he directed me to write to his friend in regard to the character of a young man residing in his (Mason's) vicinity, who had been

introduced to the ward, and who, as I understood, was somewhat smitten. Mason, as I knew,
had at one time been a teacher of stenography,
and I suggested to my employer that perhaps
his friend might send his answer to that letter
in characters that I alone could read. The idea
took at once. Although he did not say so, the
lawyer saw it would checkmate his meddlesome
daughter, and the letter was dispatched to
Mason. The answer came duly to hand, and I
will never forget the look of blank dismay, if
not disgust, on the daughter's face, as she brought
up the open stenographic letter to her father. It
was as follows : (*See page* 245.)

I translated it this way : "In reply to yours
of the 12th, I have made inquiry as to the standing of the party, which is not altogether satisfactory. As I am informed, the younger brother
is a liar (I do not vouch for this at all), he
himself, though not a professional in the best
sense of the word, has charge of a gang of
burglars, and is, in my opinion, an agent having
entree into the best houses here, and the mother
is a woman addicted to drink.

Deep in the fountains of knowledge as you
are now, do what you deem best in the premises.
He has invited your ward to the elite social this
evening, and I have consented.

Your old friend,

J. L. MASON."

Well, you had better believe that after that
endorsement the old fellow was red hot. A
sharp letter was immediately sent to Mason or-
dering him to seclude the girl and positively
prohibiting any intercourse between the young

people at all.   It ended by requesting the ward
to return at once and contained a pertinent post-
script suggesting to Mason the advisability of
keeping designing scoundrels out of his house.

An hour before train time the lawyer was at
the station despite the fact that he had so per-
emptorily ordered his ward home.

She passed him at some place on the road and
as he failed to find her waiting to receive him at
the porch of his friend's house as usual, he at
once jumped to the conclusion that the "scoundrel " had run off with her.

Darting into Mason's parlor he blurted out :
" Where is my ward, sir ? "   His offensive tone
was a surprise to the other who answered in
kind : " What do you mean, sir? "   The lawyer
retorted : " Oh, this is your friendship for me,
exposing my dead sister's child to the wiles of a
burglar and one of a family of criminals and
drunkards—you old deceiver ! "

Human nature could not stand this ; Mason
retorted hotly.   They bandied hard words
and epithets without explanation.   " Deceiver,"
" Idiot," " Old Reprobate " and " Scoundrel "
were the common expressions.   One word followed another, and the two old fellows finally
" squared off," and came to blows.   As I was
afterwards informed they wrestled around that
room and broke nearly four hundred dollars'
worth of bric-a-brac in the struggle.   It took
them four days to get over it.   See this ? "

The tramp lifted the matted hair from the
back of his head and exhibited a long white
spot.

" I got that when I went down the stairs."

"Wasn't that an odd way to travel?" the Coroner asked.

"Well, I went quick—it was a good way to get ahead. You see I got one."

The fact is, I most "busted" love's young dream by mistranslating, as anybody might, a few words in the letter. It was all the fault of the writer, not mine, though I was made the scapegoat.

This is what Mason claims he wrote :

"The younger brother is a lawyer, etc. He himself, though not a professional in the best sense of the word, has charge of a gang of brick-layers, and is in my opinion a gentleman having entree into the best houses here ; and the mother is a woman educated to drink deep in the fountains of knowledge as you are. Now, do what you deem best, etc." He explained that "which is not satisfactory " referred not to the standing of the party, but to his inquiry.

It seems the fellow referred to was a prominent builder of good family and quite a catch for the ward. The girl almost lost him and I suffered for it as you see. I have forgiven the assault on me but nevertheless got "chucked." I may say therefore that I was knocked out of the short hand profession. Nor am I sorry ; there are too many uncertainties in it for my taste— allow me, please, to warm this poker once more. I was in that case the victim of circumstances.

I then tackled newspaper work and became a veritable Bohemian. It was not unlike the easy, careless, untramelled life of a free-born American citizen such as I now enjoy. Incidentally I gave a stockholder of the company that published the paper on which I was employed, just what he deserved, and I got cashiered.

The victim was at hand to meet the circumstances as usual.

Subsequently I was told by a friend that there would be a snug berth in a certain department for anyone who would pass the Civil Service examination. I tried it. But during my previous connection with the press in an evil hour, as it was the fashion then to ridicule the whole system of civil service examination, I took a hand in, from an Irish point of view and made the wit broad and strong ; and

THIS WAS THE STORY :

Murty McAffee, a neighbor iv me own, was telling the trouble he had with the civil service examiners. Mind you, Murty's a good a pavior as ever handled a rammer, and the poor fellow has a lot of little ones to be given the bit and sup to, and needs a job bad enough, poor man ; so up he goes to pass his examination before them fellows. Seeing he was a pavior, the first question they axed him was, "What's the proper weight of a stone?"

"Why;" said Murty, "where I kem from, fourteen pounds goes to a stone." So the examiners smiled, and one of them said : " That's one point agin you, Mr. Patrick." Then said another one : " Do you know anything about Troy weight?"

"Faith, I do, sir," says Murty. " I worked on the West Shore road, with other decent men, when it was built, and I had a good long wait at Troy for me hard earnin's."

"Well," said the examiner, "can you tell us how many ounces in a pound of Troy weight?"

"Indeed, sir," says Murty, "two half-pounds weight, of eight ounces each, will do it."

"Yer out agin," says the examiner. "That is another percentage agin you." So me poor Murty got vexed, and small blame to him, and says he, purty hot like, "I know it's sixteen ounces be Brooklyn weight, and be New York weight, but if yer going to regulate the givin' of work to a man here, or fix the weight of things here be the weight of things in Troy and Albany, and them forrin parts, you can keep your ould job. There's no home rule in that," and he started to leave.

"Hould on there," says another of the examiners. "You have one more chance yet, me good man. How much in a pourd whe~e ~ou came from?"

"Twenty shillings," says Murty, and the examiners started to laugh till they were crying.

Murty got be the door, and says he: "Gintlemen, I answer the question now. You asked me what's in a pound, and I'll teli you, on me oath, I often seen better lookin' and better behaved dogs in a pound than any of yez, and their owners wouldn't bother their heads to give fifty cents apiece to take them out." And then Murty had all the laugh to himself. You see, he was a Fardown, and he didn't let it go with them so aisy.

The examiners, somehow or other, discovered that I was the author.

"Did you pass?" said the Host, as he recovered composure.

"Pass! O Lord, no. It was as much as my life was worth to pass one of the commissioners on the street, long after that; and you readily perceive that again the Victim had a disastrous collision with the Circumstances."

"You have seen many ups and downs in your life-battle," observed the Coroner, kindly.

"Aye," answered the Victim. "I could talk

to you steadily for five hours, without a break. (At this the Lawyer looked uneasily towards the door.) But what is the use?" the Stranger went on. "Yet, talking about battles, I may say I saw the field of the greatest of modern times."

"Indeed," said the Engineer. "Now you are coming to something interesting. When? what? and where?"

"Gettysburg," said the Tramp, solemnly. "I walked by that field on June 29th, two days before the carnage. I did not see the murder being done, but the field, afterwards. I was not a hero that went in to kill his fellow men; not a hired assassin; not a soldier; not even that most spiritless creature called a substitute, bought by the coward who so patriotically shed his blood —by proxy.

"An humble citizen of the world was I; aye, tramp, if you will, yet I made no widows or orphans during that awful struggle.

"Gentlemen," continued the stranger, impressively, "rising generations will never know, and can scarcely imagine the awful scenes witnessed, the dreadful things enacted—can have not the faintest conception of the excruciating sufferings of the wounded, the agony of the dying, after that tremendous grapple, in the summer of '63, on that bloody field.

"Those who talk the most of it saw the least of it; the best men never returned, for true it is that 'the flower of the army has enriched the southern dust.'

"A peaceful citizen, trudging alone the country road, I saw the blossoms in the peach-orchard before the limbs and boughs were splintered and riven by solid shot and shrieking shell.

"I beheld the white wheat-stalks waving in that memorable field, ere they were trodden beneath the feet of maddened horses and demoniac men.

"The breeze that swayed the grass on 'Little Round Top' cooled my heated brow.

"My shoeless feet trod the Gettysburg road, ere the dust was laid in our people's blood.

"The valley lay smiling before me ; the undulating hills lifted their verdure-crowned caps to the sunlight, and wee chipmunks played hide-and-seek through the gaps of that old wall, the stones of which were soon dyed a deepest red.

"I beheld and appreciated the quiet restfulness of that garden spot, and, after the slaughter, I saw it again.   O, God, what a change !"   The Stranger covered his face with his grimy hands, as though to shut out the vision before his mind's eye.

"Yes, I saw it.   Would to God I had been born blind.   And, to-day, its humblest and truest heroes, those who were thrust to the front ; who left their bones to the sward and their flesh to the buzzards, are forgotten by the busy world.

"Gentlemen, I may not express myself with facility or felicity, but I do believe that at times there arises within my breast that indescribable glow or feeling experienced by the true poet and true musician— that aspiration which lifts us high above the grovelling things of earth and makes us know that even though the trail of the serpent is over us all, yet, man is only a little lower than the angels.   Pardon me once more, friends, while I essay to recite to you in my poor way a few lines of mine, which give a faint

description of what I saw on that field, entitled
Peace and War:

I.

The air was soft ; the summer breeze
  Scarce rustled the grey dried grass
And the cattle rested beneath the trees
  That skirted the mountain pass.

II.

The dust lay thick on the quivering leaves
  As adown the fierce sun glowed,
And the barn-yard fowls made a resting place
  In the soft dry loam of the road.

III.

The chirp of the merry cricket,
  The buzz of the summer fly,
The redbreast's "tweet" in the thicket,
  The catbird's piercing cry ;
The blossomed boughs of the fruit tree
  In the passing zephyrs nod,
And bend in fullest promise
  At the bid of a bounteous God.
The house dog lolls on the sheltered porch,
  The farmer sleeps in the shade ;
The winsome lark from his leafy perch
  Wooes his feathered mate in the glade.
The ripe white wheat, the tasselled corn,
  The hum of the passing bee
Betoken to all that summer is born
  And nature is lavish and free.

*   *   *   *   *   *

IV.

The resting kine in the meadows rise
  And bend their heads to the West,
The house dog growls and the silence dies
  As the farmer wakes from his rest.

V.

A faint low sound from the edge of the wood,
  Now lost—now loud and clear,
Breaks Sabbath's quiet and restful mood
  To the strained and listening ear.

VI.

Nearer and louder, the tramp of feet
  From the east and west they come,
Breaking the corn and crushing the wheat
  To the martial roll of the drum.

VII.

The measured tramp of the serried ranks,
  The crash of the yielding rail,
And stalwart soldiers in solid phalanx
  Meet in the peaceful vale.

 * * * * * *

VIII.

The last low sighs of the dying men,
  The "swish" of the bending sheaves,
The bullets' thud, the spattering blood
  That drips on the withered leaves .
Are lost in the scream of the stricken steed ;
  The boom of the Gatling gun,
The shouts and yells, the whistling shells
  That scatter and kill and stun.
And the musket shot—the bayonet clash,
  The cries of grappling men,
And the cheering shout at the onward dash
  Are echoed from valley to glen.

 * * * * * *

Oh ! on that summer's day was a victory won,
  But the grass is no longer dry,
And dead men glare at the westering sun
  With dull unlustred eye.
The road once dusty is dark and damp,
  And the sun, like a blood-red flame,
Slowly sinks in the crimsoned clouds,
  And hides its face—in shame !

The members nodded silently and approvingly as they looked at each other.

The matter-of-fact Host was the first to break the silence: "War may be distasteful—perhaps criminal in some respects, but after all isn't it admittedly a stern necessity?"

"Aye," remarked the Lawyer, "it may be. Curiously enough it has been called with the dove and the olive branch the harbinger of peace, and perhaps it deserves the appellation."

"How so," quoth the stranger.

"Because," the other answered, "it is written, War brings famine; famine brings peace; peace brings industry; industry makes plenty; plenty brings luxury; luxury makes idleness; and idleness breeds war. And thus it goes round and round; for, some now live, but all must die; thus runs the world away."

"I see," said the Stranger, with a look of deep thought in his eyes. "As my friend, Bill Shakespeare puts it, 'All the world's a stage.' Some enter and leave immediately, having travelled to the end of their journey. Others ride farther before they reach their destination. Others again make a longer trip, but all leave at one time or another. There is a constant transfer or shifting of passengers, and the stage is ever going along the road of life, passengers ever entering and ever alighting; some are forcibly ejected, as by war, so that others who are waiting on the road may have room in the vehicle.

"But, gentlemen," he went on, "while we may look very philosophically on the subject of death—with the same serene resignation with which we submit to the misfortunes of our neighbors—it ever and anon comes so close to us as to startle and shock us as when it ruthlessly breaks the ties of blood, love or friendship.

"Why should it shock or startle us?

"And why should we not be accustomed to it? Are we not told that flesh is grass, and that it is allotted for all men once to die? For this reason I think it is singular that men break faith and fealty for a mere temporary advantage. If it be true, as the great British Commoner declared, that every one had his price, how cheaply some are sold.

"Were a man assured that he could live the years of Methuslah, and could steal enough to keep him in luxury for his nine hundred and odd years, it might pay to do it, but the game is not worth the candle, for life is too short for crookedness. This plain fact is overlooked, for creatures have been known to fatten on the dishonor of those who should be nearest and dearest to them, creatures have been known ready and willing to bastardize and disinherit their brethren and kindred for gain, so that they themselves could pose before the world as wealthy.

"Indeed, we are all too apt to be swayed by the desire for riches, honor and fame, which are but dead sea fruits, and all because the world considers the individual in respect to what he has, not what he is.

"No wonder, indeed, the dying statesman exclaimed in bitterness of spirit:

"The world is a racsal.
Its wreaths are earthly flowers of fading leaves and buds,
Its fame is but a bubble, when burst 'tis only suds.

"And when one has all earth can give, what is it?

"Let him who had wisdom beyond our ken, who possessed wealth beyond the dreams of avarice and could gratify every desire of the human heart answer :

> " Vanity of vanities, King Solomon said,
> Its pleasures are fleeting, its fruits are all dead,
> Its friendship, its love, its honor, its gold,
> Each for the last is bartered and sold.
> At the bidding of kings blood flows like a torrent,
> Flesh rots on the field till the sight is abhorrent;
> Friendship's as strong as a gossamer thread,
> And love is as light as a feather.

"And will it all be remedied in the end ? Will the crookedness be straightened in the great valley of Jehosophat ?

" Is the triumph of injustice, the prosperity of chicanery, the success of meanness, and the worship of iniquity positive proof that God liveth, and that His justice endureth forever ? Is it true that after life's short and fitful fever here we will all stand before some Being to be judged according to our lights ?

"If so, well indeed for some of us that our lights are dim, so that the judgment may be less severe. Methinks it must be so and anon, even at the risk of being classed with the fool who sayeth in his heart: 'There is no God,' I am tempted to follow Lyall into the dark realm of doubt and hopelessness and say:

> "All the world over, I wonder, in lands that I never
>   have trod,
> Are the people eternally seeking for the signs and
>   steps of a God ?
> Westward across the ocean, and northward ayont the
>   snow.

Do they all stand gazing as ever, and what do the
    wisest know ?
For destiny drives us together, like deer in a pass of
    the hills,
Above us the sky, and around us the sound of the
    shot that kills ;
Pushed by a power we see not, and struck by a hand
    unknown,
We pray to the trees for shelter, and press our lips to
    a stone.
And ever the shot strikes surely, and ever the wasted
    breath
Of the praying multitude rises whose answer is only
    Death.

"The vastness—the incomprehensibility of this
subject is overpowering to any man who thinks.
We can do but one of two things, viz.: Deny it
all, or accept it all. For, unless one has what
some call Divine Faith, we can have no further
proof of the Hereafter. Even when one denies,
one cannot doubt all."

"Why not ?"

"You cannot doubt everything—if you doubt
you cannot doubt that you doubt. But after
all—and I have given the subject some thought,
I am inclined to agree with that orthodox, if
somewhat pessimistic view of the world—

"Its hopes and its triumphs, its honor and fame,
Are only the puppets of Life's little game,
    And the winner is always Death.
Shrouds have no pockets, fame is a bubble,
    Friendship a thread, and love is a trouble ;
Glory a sham, gold is but dross,
    Yet, Truth hangeth crucified ; look to the Cross
And remember what endureth well,
    Death, Judgment, Heaven or Hell."

"Aint you getting a little off the track," suggested the Engineer.

"Surely," added the quiet gentleman.

"I beg pardon," replied the speaker, "I am in-clined to fall into these digressions. I believe I was on the subject which we all must come to sooner or later—the subject of death. Ah me, 'tis now, as your clock tells me, the witching hour of twelve—the hour when it is said the dead walk in the quiet graveyards, and spirits come forth to hold communion with each other or watch over those they best loved on earth. The tears come unbidden to my eyes as I think of one true friend whose remains I saw consigned to the place in which he was born, there to min-gle with his people into dust, where he first saw the light, away down by Chesapeake Bay.

"He was my pal as we call it, my more than brother, and like myself, a citizen of the world, vulgarly called 'tramp.' We chummed together. He divided the bread, shared the shelter with me. We call it 'Whacks' in the vernacular here, 'Cahoots' below the line. One would think that having so little, there would be much more reason to hoard it, but that was not Mat's way. Indeed he gave me the choicest morsel of the food, the snuggest part of the shelter. I honestly endeavored to do the same with him. I fear that having been so long in and of the work-a-day world it was with ill-success. For, in the awful grapple for money, in the heat of the struggle, even honest men are apt to be blinded by self interest.

"He was a born philosopher, borrowing no trouble, believing that sufficient for the day was the evil thereof. Wronging no man he did to others what he would have them do unto him.

Together we enjoyed those higher flights of fancy and the pleasures of the imagination, such as are unknown to the mere common bread-winner or money-maker, whose condition and aspirations in life are so well described in the language of the poet, whom I have always called Pope Alexander the First, 'To live, to eat, to sleep, to propagate, to die."

"Christmas, as you know, was bitterly cold. Along with the blinding storm of the 24th came a fierce northwester that blew the falling particles high into the air and made huge snow drifts in the sheltered corners of the streets and alleys. We separated that afternoon, Mat and I, he suggesting that one homeless man could get a resting place where two together would be refused shelter or driven from the premises by the dogs.

" There was lodging offered to one of us at a farmhouse on the road ; Mat begged it for me, and insisted that I should accept the offer which was made by a kind old lady, and after some hesitation I bade my pal good-night, and he left me.

"I saw him never again.

"Caring not for himself, his unselfish anxiety to see me well housed relieved, then and only then self-preservation the first law of nature (sometimes, but thank God, not always), asserted itself, and leaving me comfortable, Mat made his way through the blinding blizzard to seek a resting place for himself.

"The night was bitterly inclement, but no storm could chill that big warm heart."

The Stranger muttered something about

being somewhat affected by the smoke.   Hastily
grasping the poker, he plunged it with ostenta-
tious vigor into the still bright fire, and seemingly satisfied turned to the absorbed listeners.

"Yesterday I made my way to the ———— Sta-
tion-house and asked for him.   The doorman
usually so gruff was kindly considerate.

" 'Ah, a friend of yours? Poor fellow, come.' "

Again the speaker paused and spent some
little time in getting the fire-iron in the best
possible place in the gleaming coals.   Straight-
ening up he shut his teeth hard and after an
effort or two went on.

"My old pal, Mat, lay on a bench in a cheerless, chilly cell.   The eyes were peacefully
closed; the stiffened fingers locked across the
breast.   The grim police officers of the station
and the case hardened rounders, outcasts and
criminals, spoke in whispers or walked on tip-
toe with that needless and curious fear which
some have lest a little noise should awaken the
dead who sleep forever.

"And, O! men and brethren, from the dead
fingers had been taken a bit of paper that two
nights before had been dropped through a cre-
vice in a coal box where we slept with a homeless dog!

"The gruff doorman, with hand tender and
deft as a woman's had pinned the paper on
the dead man's breast right over the big heart
that would never throb again."

Again the faltering accents of the speaker be-
tokened his deep emotion.

"The men at the station—God bless them,
treated the dead with unlooked for reverence.

It was brought up-stairs, placed in the coffin with a few flowers about the white face. Each prisoner and each wanderer was allowed to look in turn on the peaceful countenance of the dead philosopher before the lid finally shut it from view forever, and when all was over, the body was sent to his old home.

"I—I have just completed this"—the Stranger murmured as he raised his shabby rag and with great deliberation, blew his nose loudly, winked violently once or twice and stared intently at his feet in the poor attempt to pretend he was trying to recall something. At length taking some sheets of manila paper from his pocket after a sniffle or two, in a scarcely audible, but deeply pathetic voice, he read what he called, "The Tramp's Christmas:"

> The stars look down on the sleeping town,
>   With cold and cheerless ray,
> And the northern lights came down on the heights,
>   Where the drifting snow-banks lay,
> With the telegraph lines and swinging signs,
>   The wind made mournful sound
> On that Christmas night, when the snow lay white
>   And deep on the frozen ground.
> Then an ill-clad tramp saw the precinct lamp
>   Gleam out through the frosty air,
> And shuffled foot-sore to the station-house door,
>   To beg a night's shelter there.
> He crept in, ghastly pale, with a look at the rail
> And pleaded in misery and want,
> "Cap, let me stay with you—for to-night, just please do,
>   For God's sake, Cap, don't say I can't."
> The Sergeant said, "Hey? Oh, you want to stay,
>   Well, come right up here and get warm."
> "Don't mind if I do, for I'm chilled through.
>   'Tis no night to be out in a storm;

"Thanks"—his words were cut off by a deep, hol-
    low cough,
He shivered in trying to speak,
And he clutched at the chair the doorman placed
    there,
With a grip that was grimy and weak.

THE PLACE.

Then the sergeant wrote his blotter up,
    And bade the man "come roun' "
And warm himself at the roaring fire
    Before he was "sent down."
The doorman brought him coffee
    And a goodly loaf of bread,
"I'll just take a drop of this 'ere tea,
    I cannot eat," he said.
"In fact I ain't myself at all,
    Though trouble I don't borrow,
I do feel queer as I sit here,
    Think I'll go home to-morrow."

The doorman raked the fire again,
    And passed the coffee can,
And in the genial warmth
    To chat the tramp began :
"Yes, I'll go back on the railroad track,
    If I beg or beat my way,
For I'm not the same since the morning came ;
    On this cold Christmas day
One of the oddest things occurred
    That ever happened to me,
You wouldn't think I was so soft,
    But listen and you'll see."

The sergeant left the key-board,
    And lent attentive ear
To listen to the strangest tale
    He'd heard in many a year.
"It startled me," the vagrant said,
    " And what d'ye suppose I mean ?
Just a little scrap of paper
    And a bit of Christmas green."

He coughed again as if in pain,
  Pressed his hand to his breast,
Spoke earnestly and low at times,
  And at times with sneer and jest.

THE STORY.

" It's ten years ago about," he said,
  " That I left my father's house.
In a boyish huff I stole away,
  As quiet as a mouse.
I didn't care to learn a trade,
  So my folks seemed to say,
And as for working on a farm—
  Well, I wasn't built that way.
No, I didn't follow a circus,
  Nor want to be a clown,
I was just inclined to rove a bit,
  And wished to see the town,
I thought I'd be a banker
  And go home rich and show
The folks at home that I was game
  But it didn't turn out so.
I knocked around the city here,
  Got a bite whenever I could :
Then I thought I'd make a ten-strike
  And go to work for good.
I shipped on a sailing vessel
  From New York, China bound,
Because to be a banker
  You begin on the lowest round.
But I guess I got it in the neck
  When I'd struck the Neversink.
The Captain was a savage,
  The mate was worse, I think,
The men were very near as bad,
  Scoffs and jibes and blows
Was generally my portion,
  How I stood it, Heaven knows.
Being but a friendless waif,
  A homeless, wretched lad,
I was kicked and starved and beaten,

And treated awful bad ;
Indeed among the whole ship's crew,
    I could swear it by the Book,
My only friends were the Captain's dog,
    And the boy that helped the cook.
I tried to go at Hiah-So,
    Without bidding them adieu,
But to leave without the dog and Jim
    I thought would never do.
The Captain knew I'd cut and run
    If ever I got a show ;
When I prepared to leave at port
    He ordered me below.
Before I could mature my plans
    The ship set sail again,
And off we went on another trip
    Across the raging main.
I made two trips on the Neversink,
    And didn't touch the land,
And had begun to know the ropes,
    And to reef could give a hand.
But I tell you this in confidence,
    I don't say I'm a shirk,
The way I was treated aboard that boat.
    Made me hate the sight of work.
A life on the ocean wave will do
    For sailors and for fish,
But I'm for terra firma,
    Let others have their wish.
All things have an end including ropes—
    I found this out on the ship—
We made the harbor of New York,
    And I gave them all the slip.
Then I knocked about, now here, now there,
    Without keeping any log,
And who do you think I met last week ?
    Why Jim and the Captain's dog.
He took the dog and French leave, too,
    Just shortly after me,
And weren't we glad to meet again ?
    And went partners—just us three.

We slept together most every night,
   And shared each other's food ;
Generally times were fair with us,
   Sometimes not so good.
Last night, you know, was Christmas Eve,
   So we crept in an old coal box,
Curled up snug, with the dog for a rug,
   And Jim hung up the socks.
We only had two between us,
   They wouldn't hold a thing ;
But he said : ' We'll take the chances,
   And before the chime-bells ring
Someone will give us something.
   For in times like Chrisimus
It's in the air for richer folks
   To think of fellows like us.'
And sure enough, in a hole in the box
   Some passer-by, for a caper,
Dropped in a sprig of Christmas green
   Enclosed in a piece of paper.''
The vagrant paused and coughed again,
   Rubbed his mouth on his coat,
Passed his hand before his eyes,
   And resumed when he cleared his throat :
'' When I saw that sprig of holly, Cap.,
   And what that paper said,
It brought back olden memories
   Of dear ones, long since dead.''

      *   *   *   *   *   *

His voice sank to a whisper,
   The sergeant turned around,
The tramp faltered on with his story,
   The doorman stared at the ground.

'' My mother's face, in her cap of lace,
   As she bent her old grey head
To her work at night to keep things right
   When the rest were all abed.
'Twas the verse of a song *she* used to sing,
   When I was but a child,

And the air came back when I read the words,
  And *her* voice so soft and mild.
I've got the paper here, Cap.
  To carry on my way,
For I'm going home to the old place, Cap.,
  Way down by Chesapeake Bay."

He coughed again, wiped the great dark stain
  That spread o'er his lips and chin;
All was quiet then, among these three men,
  The "touch" made them all akin.

The sergeant broke the silence at last ;
  "You go with this man,
And after you've had a good night's rest
  We'll try and think out a plan
To help you along in your journey,
  And raise you a dollar or two.
Cheer up, young fellow, never say die,
  We'll try and pull you through ! "

          *   *   *   *   *   *

When morning broke the doorman spoke
  To the sergeant under his breath,
In tones of affright—"That man—last night
  Is down there cold in death ! "

Aye ! the man was dead ; on the hard board bed
  He had died in the night alone,
And like a saving strand, in the death stiffened
      hand
  Was the verse that had been thrown,
By some one who passed where the tramps slept
      fast
  With a yellow dog between.
And this was on the paper,
  Wrapped round the sprig of green :

"God rest you, merry gentlemen,
  Let nothing you dismay,
For Christ, our Lord and Saviour,
  Was born on Christmas day."

The Victim's accents were low ; there were tears in his voice "like the Scotch song." The Coroner and Northcoat looked at each other askance as the Engineer with an "Oh, pshaw," made a movement towards the door. This brought the Stenographer to his feet, with the remark that a motion to adjourn was always in order, and would be entertained, to which all assented. The Stranger drained the pitcher, as the Coroner and his friends, after a whispered consultation, "chipped in," as they called it, and the Host, after a short absence, brought in a large bundle. At that point the taciturn Real Estate Man spoke up, "I move that a vote of thanks be tendered to the speaker of the evening and that he be elected an honorary member of the Worshipers at the Shrine of Truth, and be clothed in the habiliments of the order."

The motion being put to the house, was carried with great unanimity. Despite his strenuous expostulations, the stranger was conducted to an adjoining room, whence he soon emerged, clad from head to foot in comfortable outer clothing, of which nothing was visible but a gray frieze coat and a pair of top boots. He stood before them, his unshaven face lit up with the after-glow, while his lips murmured thanks. As he grasped the hands of his generous newly-found friends, his fellow craftsmen deftly transferred a substantial looking "wad" to his reluctant hand, and the man in the frieze coat with compressed lips and moist eyes, left them on the upper step of the stoop, below which he stood silent and irresolute.

Waving his hand at the others, he said in a

choking, disjointed voice—"Good night, gentlemen—Good night, and God bless you all," and
slowly sauntered off.

The Stranger in the After-glow.

"Poor fellow, he seemed to be a man of great
taste and deep feeling," whispered the Real
Estate Man.

"O, bless you, yes," replied the Host. "You
saw that particularly when he was drinking my
beer and reading his own poems. Did you
notice also that the beer and the essay were
ended at the same time——"

"We forgot to ask him his name," said the
other, ignoring the bold sarcasm.

"No," answered the Host, "we didn't need to ; he alluded to himself in that alleged poem as Jim ; his family name is surely Jams, the full cognomen being Jim Jams, and a most unconscionable liar he is."

"I am inclined to think that is too plebeian a name for him," suggested the Engineer. "His real name is Atramental Liegner, and he is a God-forsaken bummer——"

"No," said the Stenographer, reproachfully, glancing at the others, whole folios of protest in his tear-dimmed eyes. "No, it is my firm conviction from his talk, he is what he claims to be, the Victim of Circumstances. I believe him to be a scholar. I know he is a stenographer, and hence a gentleman."

"I agree with you," said the Coroner, after a thoughtful pause, "but I don't say with which of you."

"You and I are of one mind," remarked the Lawyer.

These remarks passed as they stood on the stoop, peering through the darkness at the tall figure sauntering down the street. Below, the lamps of a drinking place shone out like beacon lights, to warn the unwary that behind and close at hand were hidden the reefs that had wrecked so many lives. Beyond the circle of light, impenetrable darkness. Here the man in the frieze coat was lost to view. Whether he failed to heed the warning and was drawn into the danger, or whether he kept on his straight narrow course, the others knew not.

But, in the silent watches of the night, in the quiet hours between cock-crow and milkmanyawp, the entertaining stranger passed from the sight of his watching friends forever, and the Worshipers at the Shrine of Truth with all due solemnity adjourned *sine die*.

3 points

of superiority
tend to keep the

REMINGTON

STANDARD
TYPEWRITER

ahead of all competitors.

Excellence of Design.

Superiority of Construction.

Ease of Manipulation.

• • •

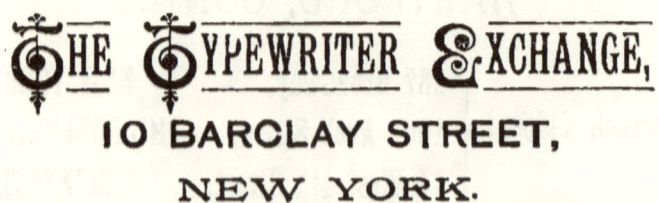

THE

LONG ISLAND
BOTTLING CO.

Cor. Third Ave. and Dean Street,

BROOKLYN, N. Y.

Long Distance Telephone, "Brooklyn, 307."

Deliver promptly to Families, Clubs, Hotels and Restaurants, the products of the

LONG ✳ ISLAND ✳ BREWERY.

Braunschweiger Mumme, (a Nutrient Tonic,)

"Black Label" Lager,

Pale Extra Lager,

Anglo-American Ale,

Porter,

WARRANTED FREE FROM
ALL ADULTERATION.

J. J. REILLY & CO.

Wholesale Dealers in

LONG ISLAND BREWERY

Fine Canada Malt Ales

AND

EXTRA BUFFALO BEER,

ALSO

Lion Brewery Pilsener and Lager Beer,

Office: 349 East 42d Street,

NEW YORK.

HAGOPIAN PHOTO-ENGRAVING CO.

Boghos Hagopian
Hazlett Gilmore } Proprietors
Theophilus Momjian

3 Great Jones St.
NEW YORK

Engraving ✦ for ✦ all Purposes
of Illustrations in Line & Half-Tone

HAGOPIAN'S NEW PROCESS

❧ C. ❀ B. ❀ L. ❧

ORGANIZED SEPTEMBER 5TH, 1881, WITH ELEVEN CHARTER MEMBERS.

Membership June 30th, 1891, - 25,659
Amount paid on death claims, -

$$\$2,655,355.88$$

COUNCILS IN (16) SIXTEEN STATES AND CANADA.

------·◆·------

Spiritual Adviser.
Rt. Rev. JOHN LOUGHLIN, Bishop of Brooklyn.
President.
JOHN C. McGUIRE.............26 Court Street.
Secretary.
JOHN D. CARROLL.........38 & 40 Court Street.
Treasurer.
WILLIAM G. ROSS..64 Water St., New York, N. Y.
Medical Examiner-in-Chief.
GEO. R. KUHN, M.D.......122 Clinton Avenue.

------◆·------

Extract from last report of State Superintendent of Insurance.

"I congratulate you on the exceptionally excellent condition of your Association—its good business methods and the uniformly honorable conduct of its affairs. It is refreshing, as well as satisfactory, to find an Association of the age of yours, and doing so large a business, using substantially all its receipts from assessments of members, without deductions, in payment of mortuary claims—paying its losses in full, and during its entire existence, having only a single contested claim out of nearly two hundred death losses."

Yours very respectfully,
R. A. MAXWELL, *Superintendent.*

THE TUXEDO,

53 CEDAR AND 25 LIBERTY STREETS,

NEW YORK CITY.

THE LEADING RESTAURANT AND OYSTER HOUSE OF DOWN TOWN.

THE CHOICEST BRANDS, MOST EFFECTIVE SERVICE, PERFECT ACCOMMADATIONS; EVERYTHING THE BEST.

· JAMES CONATY, PROPRIETOR.

The *"DENSMORE,"* the World's Greatest Typewriter, should be examined before purchasing any other. *Many Improvements.* HIGHEST STANDARD. Invented, owned and controlled by men having had fifteen years' experience on type-bar machines. *Simplicity, Strength, Durability, High Speed, Easy Action, Permanent Alignment.* Most convenient. Two interchangeable carriages. Steel throughout. *Standard Key Board with shift carriage for capitals.* Call or send for catalogue. We will appoint a reliable dealer in all cities as soon as possible, and in the meantime will ship machines on approval to parties having a good commercial rating.

"The best of all typewriters. The height of perfection. To buy any other than the *'Densmore'* is to make a mistake."

> C. T. BLUMENSCHEIN, *Stenographer*,
> National Park Bank, New York.

DENSMORE TYPEWRITER CO., 202 B'way, New York.

"EXACT GEO. R. BISHOP'S PHONOGRAPHY."

COMPLETE TEXT BOOK, adapted to SELF-INSTRUCTION, of the NEW SYSTEM with CONNECTIBLE STROKE VOWEL-SIGNS; combining UNPRECEDENTED EXACTNESS with GREAT BREVITY.

The Author, formerly a "Graham" writer, uses his "Exact" system, entirely.

EDWARD D. EASTON, Washington, D. C. (Munson Writer), who was official stenographer in the Star Route and Guiteau trials, writes: "EXACT PHONOGRAPHY is appropriately entitled. I am satisfied that by the system therein so fully set out students may learn to write shorthand with greater certainty and precision than by any of the older systems."

EDWARD B. DICKINSON, New York City, President (1887-8) N. Y. State Stenographers' Association (Benn Pittman writer), says: "He (the author) has devised a system which has in it the capacity both for the utmost exactness and for the utmost rapidity."

ISAAC S. DEMENT, of Chicago, (Graham Writer), speed contestant at N. Y. State Stenographers' Association meeting, 1887, at Alexandria Bay, says: "You have certainly captured the prize on *legibility*.

260 pp., 222 engraved. Price, bound in flexible leather, $2.00, postpaid. Circulars, Specimen Pages and Opinions of Expert Stenographers sent.

Address GEO. R. BISHOP, N. Y. Stock Exchange, New York City,

Typewriter Headquarters.

Stenographers, or any person contemplating the purchase of a Writing Machine, of any make, will find it to be to their direct interest to consult us before placing their order.

We are headquarters for the world for typewriters of all makes; at the date of writing this advertisement (Nov. 1, 1891), we have upwards of six hundred machines of all makes in our two establishments, at New York and Chicago. We supply nearly all other second-hand dealers in this country; deal with us direct and save their profit.

SOME QUOTATIONS.

Smith-Premiers, $60 to $70; Universal Hammonds, $60 to $70; Ideal Hammonds, $40 to $55; No. 1 Caligraphs, $25 to $35; No. 2 Caligraphs, $30 to $50; No. 3 Caligraphs, $45 to $60; Yosts, $50 to $70; Nationals, $30 to $40; No. 2 Remingtons, $85 to $90; No. 3 Remingtons, $85 to $95; No. 5 Remingtons, $90 to $95; Fitchs, $25 to $35; Crandalls, $20 to $40; Bar-Locks, $45 to $60; Internationals, $30 to $40; Automatics, $20 to $30; Hortons, $20 to $30; Halls, $10 to $20; Crowns, $12 to $15; Merritts, Worlds, Victors, Odells, Etc., Etc., $4 to $12. (At this writing, we have *all* of the above makes in stock *by the dozen*, and many more less popular makes.)

Persons contemplating buying a second-hand machine of any make should first consult our list of *Stolen Machines* (including ninety-three stolen Remingtons,) in order to avoid possible future trouble. We guarantee the title of every instrument purchased of us.

We ship any instrument to any part of the country, giving full privilege of thorough examination and careful trial, before accepting. After final purchase, if by any possibility full satisfaction is not had, we take back any machine purchased of us, *for full price paid*, at any time within thirty days, in exchange for any other instrument of equal or higher price desired.

We make EXCHANGING typewriters a SPECIALTY in our business; if you are not thoroughly suited, be sure and write us. We rent out machines at lowest prices to any part of the U. S.

Catalogues, illustrating and describing all machines, free on application. Courteous replies to all communications.

TYPEWRITER HEADQUARTERS,

31 & 33 Broadway, New York.   296 Wabash Avenue, Chicago.

If you want the address of any stenographer, school or shorthand, or manufacturer of typewriter anywhere in the
United States or Canada, send for **How's
Directory for Stenographers** of the
United States and Canada, handsomely
bound in cloth and gold $1.00.

THE
HOW PUBLISHING COMPANY,
TRIBUNE BUILDING,
NEW YORK, N. Y.

THE ✳ SHORTHAND ✳ REVIEW.

A JOURNAL FOR THE PROFESSIONAL REPORTER,
OFFICE STENOGRAPHER AND TYPE-
WRITER OPERATOR.

50 cents a Year.

NEW YORK,   CHICAGO,
42 Tribune Building.   415 Dearborn Street.
INDEPENDENT. REPRESENTS ALL SYSTEMS.
SEND TWO CENTS FOR SAMPLE COPY.

SCOTT-BROWNE'S ✳ MANUAL

—OF—

PITMAN ✳ PHONOGRAPHY.

1890 EDITION.

This perfected revision of the American Standard system of shorthand consists of an entire re-arrangement of the lessons and their presentation in a new and more acceptable form for class or private instruction, and

Is the cheapest book ever published for learning the art—

Because it combines the feature of a manual, phrase-book and reporters' companion, and

The whole theory of Phonography can be learned in from 15 to 20 lessons

Requiring but half the instruction necessary by former text-books.

Read these words of praise for their strength and the merit and superiority found in the system.

It stands unparalleled in the esteem of professional reporters.

You made the greatest discovery in Phonography that has yet been disclosed when you hit upon the principle of syllabication and analogy.—*C. C. Brenneman, Birmingham, Ala.*

Without running off after novelties, Mr. Scott-Browne, clearly, concisely, and in a neat and interesting manner, presents the system of Phonography which has more advocates than any other on the American continent.—*Rev. C. P. Jacobs, Clinton, S. C.*

I recommend your books because they are the best for beginners. I think your text-books are more philosophical, more uniform, and fuller than others.—*Col. Claude E. Sawyer, Official Court Stenographer, Aiken, S. C.*

Wedded as I am to the Old Phonography, I find in your volume many new and valuable principles.—*Theo. F. Shuey, of the Corps of U. S. Senate Reporters, Washington, D. C.*

I have adopted all the improvements you have introduced, and do not hesitate to commend them to every member of the profession. —*F. G. De Fontaine, Congressional Court Reporter and Journalist, New York City.*

PRICE, in handsome cloth binding, with tinted edge, **$1.50.**

Postpaid to any address.

Address, **D. L. SCOTT-BROWNE,**

AUTHOR AND PUBLISHER,

New York City, N. Y.

TO SHORTHAND WRITERS ONLY:

Would it be agreeable to you to put an extra V into your pocket three or four times a month? Nothing easier. Here is the way it is done—no interference with your regular business.

We want you to act as Agent for our Correspondence College and for the sale of our books in your neighborhood. We will appoint any reliable shorthand writer or student—one in each city and town in the United States and Canada. We publish five popular shorthand books—standard instruction books of the Pitman System. Used in nearly a hundred schools. Will give you a liberal discount; you pay for instance, $6 for one hundred Primers, retail price 25c. You also receive $5 for each student by mail you enroll for us.

Our method of teaching by mail is unquestionably the best in existence; over 4,000 students enrolled. Please send us your name with information as to yourself, and you will receive a copy of our large catalogue, with full terms to agents, and all needed information.

Address the **MORAN SHORTHAND COMPANY,**

ST. LOUIS, MO.

SHORTHAND AND BUSINESS EDUCATION.

WALWORTH

BUSINESS AND STENOGRAPHIC COLLEGE.

108, 110 EAST 125th ST.

Established in this State in 1858.

BRIEF CIRCULAR FOR 1891-2.

The President is Mr. C. A. Walworth, LL. B., associate author and part owner of Munson's Phonography, for ten years principal of the Commercial Department in the College of the City of New York, and for twenty years a business college principal. He is also editor of the "Munson News and Teacher." This is now his only school. Its stenographic department is the original MUNSON SCHOOL, and is the official headquarters for everything concerning Munson's System.

1. WHAT IS TAUGHT.

Bookkeeping of all kinds, Shorthand and Typewriting, Practical Grammar and Correspondence, Business Arithmetic, Commercial Law, Penmanship, &c., day and evening. The instruction is divided equally into two great Courses, viz.:

2. COURSES.

The BUSINESS COURSE comprises all the above branches except shorthand and typewriting. Penmanship is free in this Course. The STENOGRAPHIC COURSE comprises Shorthand, Typewriting, &c. Typewriting is free in this Course. Each Course is completed in six months. The humbug of "shorthand proficiency in three months" is not promised here, although this school can teach faster than any other.

3. PRICES.

Either Course, six months, including diploma, $70. Instalment payments accepted. Evening courses at lower prices or by allowing more weeks.

4. LADIES' DEPARTMENT.

Occupies a separate suit of rooms, carpeted and furnished expressly for such students, but no cheap women teachers are employed.

5. WHEN TO COMMENCE.

At any time, as every pupil is taught separately. Open the entire year.

6. SCHOOL HOURS.

9 A. M. to 3 P. M.   Evenings, 7.30 to 9.30.

7. BOARD FOR STRANGERS.

Good board and room procured at $5 per week.

8. SITUATIONS.

Constant demand from employers at high salaries. No similar school has half so many shorthand graduates in profitable positions, and no other school has graduates filling high positions as official stenographers in the city courts and departments, viz.: Superior Court, Park, Dock, Fire and Public Works Departments and Aqueduct Commissioners, besides thousands of law, railroad and business offices and others conducting first-class stenographers' offices on their own account. Its graduates command situations at $50 to $75 per month from the start.

The above is a complete although brief circular—cut it out. Write for a sample copy of the "Munson Monthly Phonographic News and Teacher." $2 per year, published here.

The Government Baking Powder Tests.

The latest investigations by the United States and Canadian Governments show the Royal Baking Powder a cream of tartar powder superior to all others in leavening strength. -

Statements by other manufacturers to the contrary have been declared by the official authorities falsifications of the official reports.

www.ingramcontent.com/pod-product-compliance
Lightning Source LLC
Chambersburg PA
CBHW020846020726
47497CB00005B/1272